CW00933103

CAUTION CAUTION CAUTION CAUTION

RESTRICTED
AREA

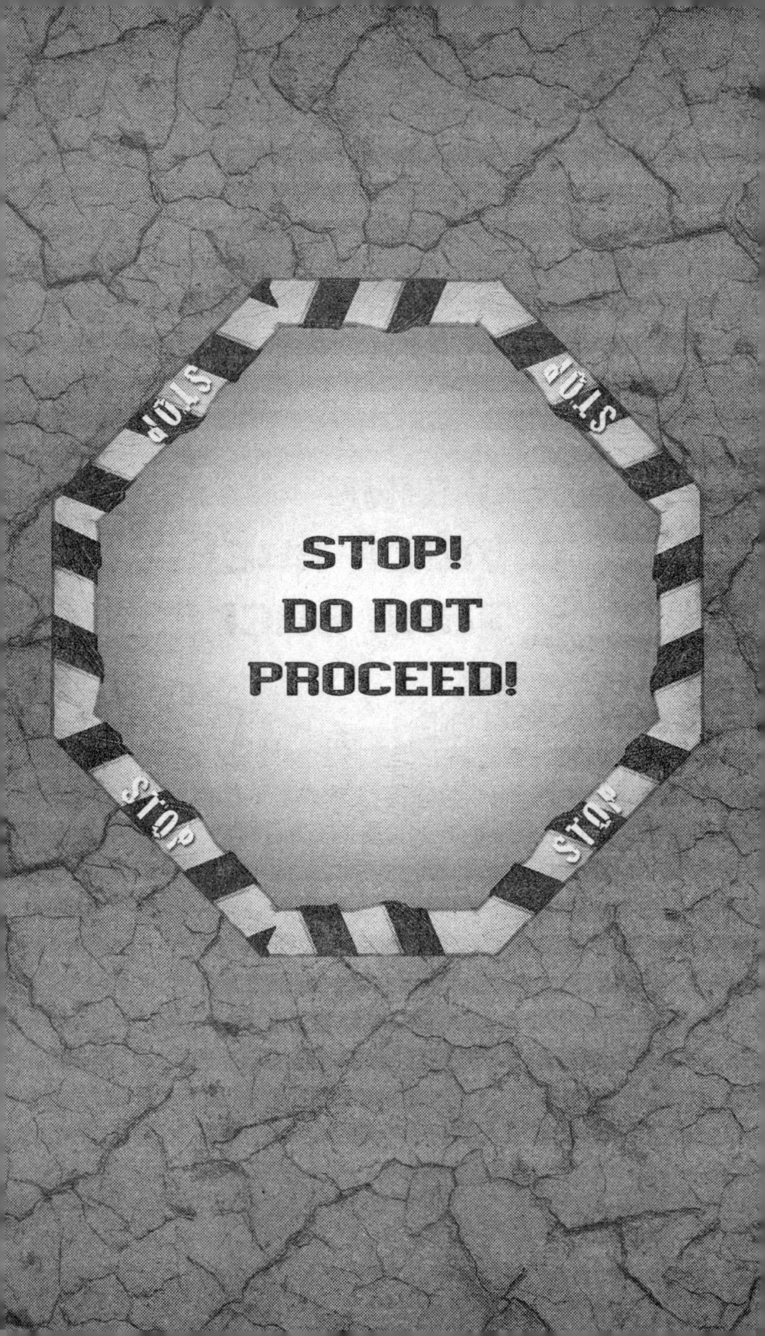
STOP!
DO NOT
PROCEED!

**YOU
HAVE BEEN
WARNED.**

JUNIOR NOVELIZATION

Adapted by Scott Ciencin

Based on a
motion picture screenplay
written by Peter Buchman

Based on the characters
created by Michael Crichton

B■XTREE

First published 2001 in the United States by Random House,
Inc., New York, and simultaneously in Canada by
Random House of Canada Limited, Toronto

First published in Great Britain 2001 by Boxtree
an imprint of Macmillan Publishers Ltd
25 Eccleston Place, London SW1W 9NF
Basingstoke and Oxford
Associated companies throughout the world
www.macmillan.com

ISBN 0 7522 1976 6

Copyright © 2001 Universal Studios Publishing Rights, a division
of Universal Studios Licensing, Inc., 2001 Jurassic Park III and
Jurassic Park Institute are trademarks and copyrights of
Universal Studios and Amblin Entertainment, Inc.

The right of Universal Studios Publishing Rights to be identified
as the authors of this work has been asserted by them in
accordance with the Copyright, Designs and Patents Act 1988.

Special thanks to Cindy Chang of Universal Studios and to
Alice Alfonsi, Jason Zamajtuk, Lisa Findlay. Michael Wortzman,
Arthur Bennett, Christopher Shea, Jenny Golub and Stephanie
Finnegan of Random House for their work on this book.

All rights reserved. No part of this publication may be
reproduced, stored in or introduced into a retrieval system, or
transmitted, in any form, or by any means (electronic, mechanical,
photocopying, recording or otherwise) without the prior written
permission of the publisher. Any person who does any
unauthorized act in relation to this publication may be liable
to criminal prosecution and civil claims for damages.

9 8 7 6 5 4 3 2 1

A CIP catalogue record for this book is available from
the British Library.

Printed and bound in Great Britain by
Mackays of Chatham PLC, Chatham, Kent

PROLOGUE

THIRTEEN-YEAR-OLD ERIC KIRBY hung high in the sky. Below him, his running shoes dangled over brilliant blue waves. Above him, a colorful parasail fluttered like a giant wing.

"This is so awesome!" Eric shouted as the wind rustled his thick brown hair and whipped through his loose red shirt. "We're going to see dinosaurs!"

Strapped beside Eric in the two-person harness, Ben Hildebrand raised his camcorder. "And we'll be able to prove it!"

Whooping with laughter, Eric took in the lush tropical coastline of Isla Sorna, 120 miles west of Costa Rica. Several years ago, genetic engineers had brought dinosaurs back to life here, hoping to create a sort of dinosaur zoo.

But Jurassic Park had never opened to the public. A number of accidental deaths had spooked the owners, and Costa Rican and United Nations authorities had declared both Isla Sorna and its companion island, Isla Nublar, a no-flying, no-boating zone.

Of course, Enrique, the driver of the Dino-Soar speedboat now towing them, didn't care about that. And neither did Eric. This was his chance to finally see *live* dinosaurs, and he was taking it!

Turning his head, Eric smiled at the man who was treating him to this adventure—Ben Hildebrand.

Ben was kind of old, at least thirty, but he was pretty cool despite that. The two of them had done a lot of exciting things together since Ben had started seeing Eric's mom—and, hey, ever since Eric's mom and dad had separated, he'd take whatever attention he could get.

Ben was an extreme-sports sort of dude, which meant he was the complete opposite of Eric's father. And that, Eric had pretty much guessed, was one of the big reasons why his mom and dad had separated. His dad had just gotten boring or something to his mom.

But Eric didn't want to think about that stuff. Not today.

The riskier the better! was Ben's motto, and Eric loved that sort of thinking. Of course, he loved his dad, too, but his supercautious father was the *last* person who'd try something as dangerous as this!

And maybe Ben was right when he said: *What does risk matter when you can live a dream come true?*

Suddenly, Eric felt a sharp tug on the towline securing them to the speedboat below.

"Whoa!" Ben yelled.

Looking down, Eric saw that the Dino-Soar tour boat had disappeared into a low bank of fog. When it emerged, there was no sign of their driver. But there was one thing they *could* see, one horrifying sight: The deck was splattered with blood!

"Ben!" Eric called.

Ben stared, gape-mouthed.

Below them, the boat was heading north, into the open ocean—and the nearest shore was a thousand miles away!

"I'm going to unclip us!" Ben called, then frantically unfastened the lines securing them to the driverless boat.

As the parasailers floated upward, a strong wind sent them wafting over the daunting cliffs of Isla Sorna.

Eric felt a terrible chill.

He was going to see dinosaurs. *Live* dinosaurs.

Only it was no longer a dream come true.

It had just become a nightmare.

CHAPTER 1

GRRRR-AHHRRRRRR!

A spike-backed Ankylosaurus smashed against the flank of a long-necked dinosaur in a suburban backyard. Plastic clicked and scraped against plastic as the child who owned the toys roared ferociously.

Dr. Alan Grant squatted next to three-year-old Charlie, watching with great delight as the little boy played in his sandbox. Ellie Satler's pretty face smiled down at the two. She held an infant in her slender arms. The group looked like a perfect family.

"Actually, Charlie, those two are herbivores," Alan said, squinting in the harsh late afternoon sunlight. "They eat plants. They wouldn't be interested in fighting each other. But these—"

The paleontologist picked up a plastic Tyrannosaurus rex and a Carnotaurus. "See, Charlie, *these* are carnivores," he said. "They eat meat. This one here—see its claws—this one here uses its claws to gouge out the throat of its opponent."

Alan demonstrated with some grunts and groans of his own. Charlie's eyes went wide with fright.

"Uh, Alan?" Ellie said.

"Hmm?" Alan said.

"He's *three,*" Ellie reminded him. "Why don't you wait till he's five?"

"Oh, right," Alan said. He made the dinosaurs do a little dance along the edge of the sandbox. "Happy dinosaurs!"

Alan heard a car engine turn off and a door slam.

"That must be Mark," Ellie said. She turned and called out, "Mark, we're back here!"

Alan and Ellie turned to see Mark Degler come through the gate carrying a briefcase. He appeared handsome and friendly, and his suit looked as if it cost more than Alan made in an entire month.

Mark and Ellie kissed tenderly on the lips.

Alan tensed.

"Good day at the State Department?" Ellie asked.

"Keeping the world safe," Mark said. He gestured to the baby. "Here, let me take him."

Ellie gently handed him the baby. "Mark, this is Alan Grant."

"Nice to meet you, Alan," Mark said. He

cradled the baby against him with one hand and held out his other hand. "I've heard a lot about you."

Alan shook the outstretched hand. He felt like an outsider. There had been a time when he belonged here, in Ellie's life. But that time was past.

"Daddy, this is a herbabore," Charlie said, holding up a toy dinosaur. "And that's the dinosaur man."

Alan smiled uncomfortably.

After dinner, Ellie walked Alan to his rented car. Night had fallen and Mark was putting Charlie to sleep.

"You didn't talk shop much," Ellie said. "That's not like you."

Alan shrugged. "Mark didn't seem like the type to be interested in scientific theories and fund-raising tours."

"Well, I am," she said. "What's been happening?"

They stopped by his car and leaned against the doors.

"Raising money was never easy," Alan said. "But before Jurassic Park became worldwide news, you could at least find it. Somewhere. Now fossils are out. Everyone wants to see real live dinosaurs."

Ellie nodded.

"I've found raptor remains at my new site," said Alan. "I have a theory that the key to their social intelligence, the way they can work together as a team, lies in their ability to talk to each other."

Ellie shuddered. "You mean those sounds they made."

"Given a chance, I'm certain I can prove my theory that the raptor might have been capable of birdlike vocalizations," Alan said. He pushed away from the door and got inside. "Given a chance . . ."

He rolled down the window and Ellie crouched beside it.

"Times change, Alan," Ellie said. "But you're still the best. I mean that."

"The last of my breed." Alan looked away. "I'd better get going."

"Let me know if I can help, Alan," Ellie said. "You're bad about asking for help, but *please ask me*. Anything, anytime."

Alan nodded reassuringly as he turned the key in the ignition. He didn't want Ellie to worry about him. Ellie was happy with the life she had chosen. Maybe if things had been different, if *he* had been different, he might have been the one to share that life with her.

But he hadn't been ready to make that

commitment, and he still wasn't. Not to her, not to anyone. Not when there was so much work to be done.

Paleontology, the focus of his entire life, stood on the brink of extinction. Many believed that all dinosaur scientists had to do now was travel to Isla Sorna or Isla Nublar—the two Jurassic Park sites—and study the living dinosaurs there. But Alan knew different.

Dinosaurs, *true* dinosaurs, lived 65 million years ago. The answers to how they lived were in the fossil record—*not* in the genetically engineered theme-park monsters that John Hammond and InGen had created for profit.

Alan was one of the few scientists still dedicated to keeping the study of fossils from perishing. His career *had* to come first.

Ellie touched his hand. "When I met you, I thought that millions of years ago, all the dinosaurs became extinct. Wiped out. But you told me otherwise. When conditions changed, dinosaurs became other things. They evolved."

"A well-accepted theory," Alan said.

Ellie stared at him for a long moment. He could feel the love they would always share.

"Alan," she said with a seriousness he hadn't expected, "don't be afraid to evolve."

* * *

The next morning, Alan arrived at the excavation base camp in Fort Peck Lake, Montana. He found Billy Brennan, an associate professor and site manager, working his charm on Cheryl. She was one of a dozen college students at the site.

"Dr. Grant!" Billy said as he quickly moved away from Cheryl and took one of the heavy bags Alan carried. Another was slung over Alan's shoulder.

"How was your trip?" Billy asked. "Did you get the funding we need to keep the site going?"

Alan shook his head. "We'll be broke in four weeks."

"Three weeks," Billy said cheerfully. "I had to rent some equipment."

They left the glaring sun behind and entered one of the many tents making up the camp. The new equipment Billy had mentioned was on a nearby table. Alan frowned as he took in the dusty Macintosh feeding information to a squat mechanism the size of a small refrigerator. An arm stuck out from the machine and swept back and forth across a block of resinlike material.

"Meet the future of paleontology," said Billy.

"Oh, yeah? Can it dig?" asked Alan. He hated technology.

"It's a rapid prototyper," Billy said with patience. "I feed in the scan data from the raptor skull; the computer breaks it into thousands of slices; and this thing sculpts it, one layer at a time."

The machine's arm stopped suddenly. Billy lifted a hinged top cover, reached inside, and carefully broke loose a hollowed-out object the size of a man's fist. Shaking out the remaining dust, he raised the object into the afternoon light as if it were the Holy Grail.

"I give you the resonating chamber of a Velociraptor!" Billy said proudly.

"Don't you mean the *computer-simulated* resonating chamber of a Velociraptor?" Alan corrected.

"Whatever! Okay, now listen to this." Billy put the chamber to his lips and blew through it as if it were a conch shell.

Hrrrr-reeeeee!

The sound it made was unique and piercing, the cry of an ancient animal. A nearby flock of birds immediately leaped into frightened flight.

A shudder of memory sliced through Alan. The last time he'd heard that call was eight years ago on Jurassic Park. He'd almost been ripped to shreds by raptors.

Shrugging off the memory, Alan focused instead on his talented student. Billy continued to blow into the chamber, changing the pitch and trying different types of calls.

"This is brilliant, Billy," said Alan, truly amazed at the feat. "But I'm afraid it's a little late."

Looking past Alan, Billy noticed some activity beyond the tent. A Cadillac SUV had pulled up and a couple was getting out.

"Oh, I forgot to tell you," said Billy, watching Cheryl point the man and woman toward the tent. "Some amateurs wanted to come by and talk with you. I told them you'd be happy to chat with them."

Alan's good mood faded. "Absolutely not. We have little enough time as it is."

"Too late," Billy said.

"What?" Alan looked over and saw the newcomers.

"Dr. Grant?" the man asked, approaching him.

"Yes?"

"Paul Kirby. Kirby Enterprises." Paul reached into his breast pocket and produced an impressive business card.

Alan placed the resonating chamber in his pack—he'd examine it more closely later. Then he took Paul Kirby's card and looked it over. The card told him almost nothing—except that money had been spent on it.

"And this is my wife, Amanda," Paul said.

Amanda shook Alan's hand and smiled. She looked tired.

"What can I do for you, Mr. Kirby?" asked Alan tightly.

"Well, sir, I am a great admirer of yours and have an *extremely* interesting proposition to discuss. Would you let my wife and me take you to dinner? Our treat."

"Maybe some other time," said Alan.

"I guarantee it'll be worth your while," insisted Paul.

Behind him, Billy rubbed his thumb and index finger together to indicate that these people were *rich*.

Growling inwardly, Alan mustered a weak smile. "It'd be my pleasure."

An hour later, Alan and Billy were ordering dinner at a local bar and grill. Paul and Amanda sat across the table.

"Amanda and I, well, we just love the outdoors," Paul said. "We love adventure. Galápagos, K2, the Nile. You name it, we've done it."

"We even have two seats reserved aboard the first commercial moon flight," Amanda proudly added.

"Hmmm," grunted Alan, far from impressed.

"Now, for our wedding anniversary this year,

we want to do something really special, something once-in-a-lifetime," Paul said. "So we've arranged for a private airplane to fly us over Isla Sorna. And we want you to be our guide."

Alan winced. The Kirbys were looking at him as if they had just offered him an amazing gift.

He sighed. "I'm sorry, but there's no force on Earth or in heaven that could get me anywhere near InGen's creations again. I can give you a list of *other* paleontologists you might call."

"But you're the best," Paul said insistently. "You've seen these animals in the flesh. No one can come close to you."

Alan sighed. Paul was a talkative, cheerful fellow who seemed to have no "off" switch. Alan knew the type. Unfortunately, Paul's species was in no danger of extinction.

"No," Alan said. "Besides, with the air restrictions after that T. rex incident in San Diego four years ago, you can't fly low enough to see anything of interest."

Paul frowned. He was clearly not used to people saying no.

"We have *permission* to fly low," Amanda said.

"How low?" Billy asked.

"Well, I'm no expert on flying," Paul said. "But I do know it's a lot lower than anyone else."

"We can fly as low as we want," Amanda said.

"Paul's made some connections through his business. Especially in the Costa Rican government."

Paul pulled out his checkbook. "I'm prepared to make a sizable contribution to your research, Dr. Grant."

Billy's eyes widened, urging Alan: *Don't say no!*

"I can write all kinds of numbers on this check," Paul said with a smile. "Just tell me what, exactly, it would take."

Alan looked away. *How could it have come down to a choice like this?*

He had vowed never to return to that area. But if he didn't, then his dig would end before he proved his theory. He was so close, too. So close to showing why paleontologists were still needed, even in this new world of "living dinosaurs."

I'm out of money, realized Alan. *And out of options.*

CHAPTER 2

ALAN TRIED AND FAILED to get comfortable in his cramped seat. The Kirbys had chartered a Beechcraft Turboprop for their sight-seeing trip, and the small plane was now cruising along through clear blue skies.

Across from Alan, Billy cleaned his camera lenses, then put them away in a sad-looking case.

"Even with what I pay you, you could get a better bag," Alan said.

"No way," said Billy, holding up the ragged camera bag. "This one is lucky. Couple years ago, some buddies and I went hang gliding off these cliffs in New Zealand. Updraft sent me right into the side. BOOM! It was this strap alone that saved my life. Got caught on a rock as I was falling."

"Ah, reverse Darwinism," Alan teased. "Survival of the most idiotic."

Billy laughed. "Listen, Alan, I really appreciate you bringing me along."

"The fossils will be there when we get

back," Alan said with a shrug. "That's the nice thing about bones. They never run away. And besides, you got me into this."

Alan sat back and tilted his hat over his eyes. The calm, steady humming of the plane's engines soon put him to sleep. Hours later, a bump woke him with a start. He glanced out the window, but clouds obscured his view.

Suddenly, the clouds parted to reveal Isla Sorna rising majestically out of the water. It seemed impossibly green and lush after the dry brown landscape around their Montana dig.

"Admit it," Billy said. "You're excited."

"I'll admit no such thing," Alan whispered as he rubbed the sleep from his eyes and stifled a yawn.

The plane descended sharply to the island and leveled out a hundred feet above the treetops.

Alan spotted a dinosaur below. He was surprised to feel his heart beating faster.

"There!" Alan said, pointing to a long-necked dinosaur lumbering along a clearing. "It's an apatosaur. Look at the coloration."

Billy was amazed. "I—I'm so used to just seeing bones. It's weird to see skin. Wow . . ."

Alan wasn't surprised to hear the awe in Billy's voice. He well remembered how stunned and overwhelmed he himself had felt the first time he'd seen one of InGen's creations.

For Alan, it had felt as if the past had come alive. But now Alan knew the truth. These dinosaurs were never meant to coexist with man. They had brought only pain and death. And since that awful trip eight years ago, Alan had vowed to forget the wonder he'd first experienced in Jurassic Park.

Even at this distance, he refused to let his guard down.

So do your tour-guide duty and get the heck out of here, he told himself, noticing that Paul and Amanda weren't even looking out the window.

"Mr. and Mrs. Kirby!" Alan called toward the front. "If you look out the right, you can see—"

Paul waved him away. Alan exchanged looks with Billy.

"Weird," Billy whispered. "But I get the feeling they're not getting along too well. Seems like one of those second honeymoons to save the marriage, you know?"

Alan looked back to the window. Everyone on the flight had been strangely quiet ever since they'd taken off. The pilot and copilot were hardly friendly, and the "steward," a stern-looking man with dark glasses, sat rigid a few rows back.

All three of them, the pilot, copilot, and steward, wore matching outfits: black slacks and

T-shirts, leather boots, and expensive silver watches. Something about all three of them made Alan feel uneasy, though he couldn't say why.

Suddenly, Alan heard a mechanical hum and a low rush from outside. His lungs stilled. "That's *not* the landing gear?"

Paul, Amanda, and the steward didn't respond.

"You can't *land*." Alan stared, unable to believe this was happening.

Paul turned back to him. "Dr. Grant, if you'll just sit tight, we'll explain this all in a jiffy."

"This plane cannot land!" Bolting from his seat, Alan sprang toward the cockpit. He would wrestle the controls from the pilot if he had to!

The steward grabbed Alan and pulled him back. Alan started to struggle, but a well-placed fist struck him and his world went dark.

"Eric! Eric! Are you there, honey? Ben! *Eric!*"

It was Amanda Kirby's voice. Alan realized that much as his blurry vision cleared and he came around.

He was lying on the floor of the plane. His head was pounding as Billy helped him up.

"Tell me we didn't land," Alan said.

Billy was silent. Clearly, he didn't want to lie to his mentor. "I think they're looking for someone," Billy said.

Billy helped Alan to the exit door, then down the steps. The small plane was parked at one end of a rutted and vine-covered landing strip that the jungle had nearly reclaimed.

The pilot, copilot, and steward were checking a cache of weapons. Alan's heart sank. Clearly, these three fools had no idea what they were up against.

Paul Kirby trotted over. "Dr. Grant, are you all right? I'm so sorry that Mr. Cooper had to be so, well . . ."

Alan's gaze followed the trio of armed men until they disappeared into the trees and brush. "What's going on? What are they doing?"

"Mr. Udesky—he's team leader," Paul said. "He, Mr. Nash, and Mr. Cooper are establishing a perimeter. Making it safe. These guys are really good. One of them was a Green Beret, and—"

Alan cut him off. "Mr. Kirby, trust me. On this island, there is no such thing as *safe*. We have to get back in this plane."

"ERIC!"

Alan turned to find Amanda standing on the edge of the runway, calling into the jungle with a bullhorn.

"At least tell your wife to stop making so much noise!" Alan said. "We're *food* to the animals who live here!"

Paul cupped his hands over his mouth. "Amanda! Honey! Dr. Grant says it's a bad idea!"

With the bullhorn, Amanda called, "What?"

Paul pointed at Alan. "He says it's a *bad idea!*"

Amanda shouted into the bullhorn. "*What's* a bad idea?"

Suddenly, a deafening roar came from the jungle. Everyone turned toward the sound and froze.

Paul looked to Alan. "What was that?"

Billy took a step back and whispered, "Is it a rex?"

"I don't think so," answered Alan.

Paul and Billy breathed a sigh of relief.

"Sounds *bigger,*" Alan said.

A rustling came from the nearby brush. Udesky and Nash suddenly sprinted out of the jungle and headed for the plane.

"We gotta go!" Udesky called.

Paul didn't look at all pleased. "What's the problem? Can't you guys—"

"Everyone in the plane!" Udesky commanded. "*Now!*"

CHAPTER 3

ALAN RAN FOR THE PLANE, taking the stairs three at a time. He quickly grabbed a seat and watched Nash rush toward the cockpit. The others scrambled on board, then secured their seat belts as Udesky slammed the door shut.

"We can't just *leave!*" Amanda told her husband.

"Don't worry, honey," Paul said, taking her hand. "We'll circle around and come back."

Near the door, Billy confronted Udesky. "What about the other guy?"

"Coop's a professional," Udesky said. "He can handle himself."

Suddenly, a bloodcurdling scream echoed through the jungle, followed by bursts of machine-gun fire. Alan looked through his window, but he couldn't see anything.

From the cockpit, Nash yelled, "We're going!"

Udesky turned from Billy and stormed

forward, climbing into the copilot's seat as Nash revved the engine.

Clearly upset, Billy looked to Alan for some guidance.

"Sit down and strap yourself in," said Alan as the plane started moving. "There's nothing either of us can do."

The passengers bounced in their seats as the plane quickly picked up speed along the rugged, overgrown runway strip.

Alan leaned toward the aisle and took in the view through the cockpit's front window. Two hundred yards ahead of the plane, a figure emerged from the jungle. It was Cooper. He stood in the middle of the runway, waving one arm wildly. His other arm, badly injured, hung limp by his side.

Udesky and Nash exchanged serious looks.

"Coop, you know I can't do it, pal," Nash said. He slammed the throttle open full. He had to reach flying speed.

A few rows ahead of Alan, Paul gripped his seat's armrest and called, "What are you doing? You have to stop! That's Mr. Cooper!"

On the runway, a shadow fell over the injured mercenary. Then, with brutal speed, an enormous beast seized him up in its massive jaws and lifted him into the air. Alan saw only a glimpse of a long crocodilian snout, powerful clawed forearms, and a spiny sail rising from the creature's back. Then the plane rose and appeared to clear the dinosaur.

Suddenly, there was an angry roar and a shuddering thump. The out-of-control turboprop banked into the jungle as Alan and all the passengers were thrown about.

We're going to crash! Alan realized. He gripped the armrests as the craft tore through the trees, losing a wing and pieces of its tail. Every impact was explosive.

The plane finally came to rest in the jungle canopy and settled in the tree branches.

Alan's breathing was quick and shallow. He looked around. No one seemed hurt.

"The cockpit radio is dead," Udesky called. "Nash, get the sat-phone from Kirby."

Paul handed the satellite phone to Nash, who dialed out.

"We're sorry, all circuits are busy," said a prerecorded voice. "Please try your call again later."

Alan unstrapped himself, climbed back to the side door, and shoved. The door opened partially, revealing a thirty-foot drop to the jungle floor! With a gasp, Alan quickly closed and latched the door.

A few feet away, Amanda screamed. Alan turned in time to see a huge reptilian face appear in the cockpit window, its maw open wide. Claws ripped through the thin hull and the plane was yanked from side to side.

This time, Amanda wasn't the only one who screamed.

Then the claws disappeared and the plane settled into the tree branches once more. The attack had ended as suddenly as it had started.

"Guess it's not in the mood for sardines in a can," Paul whispered.

Amanda stared at him, clearly appalled that he could joke at a time like this!

Nash and Udesky still sat in the cockpit. They squirmed in their seats as the dinosaur reappeared in the cockpit window.

"Get out of there!" Alan yelled to them.

The mercenaries were struggling with their seat belts as the dinosaur tore the nose off the plane, leaving them sitting in open air.

Alan felt his stomach lurch as the front of the plane tilted downward. The jungle floor was visible far below.

Udesky unbuckled his seat belt and lunged back toward the cabin. Nash tried to follow, but a long snout clamped down on his leg.

Alan saw Nash get pulled out of the plane—then he heard the man's screams.

As Udesky climbed farther back into the passenger section, he lost his grip and started to slide back toward the front of the plane. Alan grabbed his arm just in time!

Rhhhhhhrrrr-ghrrrrr!

A mammoth snout jammed itself into the body of the airplane. Powerful jaws opened, dripping with saliva. The dinosaur lunged for Amanda, its eyes wide and burning with hunger! She pulled her dangling legs back, barely escaping the daggerlike teeth as the jaws snapped shut.

Billy unbuckled Amanda's seat belt and, with Paul's help, hauled her up into the next row back.

Then everyone scrambled to the back of the plane. The dinosaur suddenly withdrew, and the shift in weight sent the fuselage tipping backward and falling to the jungle floor!

The wreckage flipped as it fell, and Alan and the other bruised passengers came to rest sprawled on the ceiling of the plane.

For a few seconds, everything was quiet. Then a huge eye appeared in the window and the plane was *slammed* across the jungle clearing!

Inside, the passengers were hammered against the walls of the plane, tumbling like socks in a dryer. Debris, seats, and luggage flew everywhere!

They finally came to an abrupt stop when the plane smashed into a tree.

Loud thumps gradually drew closer, and then

a giant foot stepped on what was left of the metal fuselage, flattening it like a paper tube.

"This way!" yelled Alan as a huge claw started to peel the plane open. He led the group out the open end of the plane and urged them into the jungle.

As a tremendous roar came from behind them, Alan saw his assistant stop dead in his tracks.

Billy stared speechless as he stole a glimpse at the dinosaur that had attacked them. It had a dark, horrible shape and a strange mix of features that few dinosaurs possessed—and it was coming right for them!

With a groan of frustration, Alan raced toward his awestruck assistant and yanked him into the jungle.

CHAPTER 4

ALAN'S HEART RACED as he led the group through the jungle.

The thunderous footfalls of the dinosaur grew louder as it bore down on the group. The ground shuddered and quaked.

Crrr-accckkk!

A young tree toppled to Alan's left as the dinosaur smashed through the jungle. It was almost upon them!

They passed through the underbrush. Ahead was a thick grove of large trees with wide trunks.

There! Alan thought. *The dinosaur won't be able to fit between the trunks!*

Alan led the group through the narrow gaps between the trees. Behind him, he heard a thud that made the ground seem to vibrate.

Rrrrhhhh-gahhhrrrr!

Alan sighed with relief as he heard the dinosaur's roar of frustration. It had run up against one of the thicker trees and bounced off. It could not follow its prey.

"Come on, keep moving!" Alan demanded. Determined to get as far away from the dinosaur as possible, he led the others at a breathless pace through the grove. The spaces between the trees finally widened, and Alan directed them into a clearing.

Then he stopped dead and everyone halted behind him, all of them gasping for breath. At the center of the clearing lay a mass of scales the size of a house.

Alan tensed—until he identified the animal. It was an immense, unmoving sauropod. A plant-eating long-neck. Harmless—so long as it didn't charge at you, step on you, or smack you with its tail.

The dinosaur lay on its side, its eyes wide and unseeing.

"Don't worry," Alan said. "It's dead."

The sauropod looked like a Datousaurus, a fifty-foot-long Middle Jurassic herbivore whose fossils were found in the Dashanpu Quarry of central China. Datousaurus lived in well-watered lowland. But . . .

How could a dinosaur that large even make it into this clearing—unless there was another way in he hadn't spotted?

With a low, shuddering growl, a full-grown bull Tyrannosaurus rex rose up from behind the carcass. It had been feeding on the plant-eater.

Alan heard gasps of fear behind him.

"Nobody move a muscle," Alan said. "A rex tracks motion."

Alan stood perfectly still as the rex moved its head from side to side. Searching. The gigantic predator sniffed the air and growled in frustration.

Alan knew that a rex could pick up a scent from miles away. The small group smelled of soap. Aftershave. Perfume. Human sweat. Alien scents for this environment. But the carcass of the dead animal also had a scent—a rather bad one. So long as no one moved—

A scuffling made Alan look back. "Oh, no . . . ," he whispered in horror.

Udesky was *running*!

Alan's gaze went back to the rex. The predator swiveled its head in the mercenary's direction. The dinosaur's eyes blazed. Fresh meat was clearly preferable to an old carcass.

GRRRR-AHHHHRRRRR! the rex roared. Then it stomped toward the humans with earth-shaking footfalls.

Alan spun and saw Paul and Amanda take off with Billy after the mercenary. He ran after them, the rex on his heels!

They darted between the heavy trees, back the way they had just come. The rex *squeezed* through the spaces behind them. Smashing branches and wailing in rage and frustration, the predator was slowed in its pursuit of its prey.

Slowed, but not stopped.

Alan leaped over low-lying branches, darted around muddy ruts in the earth, and headed straight for the golden beams of sunlight breaking through the far end of the thick forest. Behind him, the rex smashed and crashed through the grove, gaining on him with every step.

Ahead, Billy and the others were breaking through the cluster of heavy trees. The sun nearly blinded Alan as he joined them, wondering why they had come to a stop.

Then he saw why.

A shape was towering over them, blocking the sun. The nightmare black form outlined a dinosaur even bigger than the rex behind them.

Talk about reverse Darwinism! Alan realized in frustration. This group of "intelligent" omnivores had just delivered themselves to the sail-backed predator they'd fled from in the first place!

The dinosaur was nearly fifty feet long and over sixteen feet high. A bony sail lined its back, and its head was crocodilian, with rows of curving teeth. Sinewy, long arms extended, revealing three-fingered hands with fourteen-inch claws. The animal reached toward Paul, the closest of the gaping, speechless humans.

Suddenly, a crash and a roar sounded from the trees behind them. The sail-back lifted its head toward the approaching rex—and let out a threatening roar.

Good! Alan thought. *Let them fight it out to see who gets to eat us. We can be long gone before they're finished!*

"Go," Alan said to the others. "Go now! Move!"

The group scattered. Paul and Amanda went in one direction, Billy and Udesky the other. Alan moved to join his assistant and the mercenary in the brush—but something grabbed hold of his leg!

Looking down, Alan saw that his right foot was stuck in a tangle of branches. From one direction, the rex raced toward him, maw wide, claws clicking with anticipation. From the other direction, the sail-back was flying forward.

Trapped between the two predators, Alan suddenly knew what it felt like to be a football on the fifty-yard line of the Super Bowl!

Dropping to one knee, Alan pulled at the branches with all his strength. They opened just wide enough for him to yank out his foot.

As two great shadows fell over him, Alan dove for cover between a pair of massive logs. Above him, the rex and the sail-back rammed into each other, and the ground quaked and shuddered beneath him. The jarring impact rattled every bone in his body!

Lying flat on his back, Alan let out a terrified gasp as the sail-back's giant foot suddenly landed across the two tree trunks. The foot had been stopped just a few inches above his face!

The sail-back attacked the T. rex a second time, but the rex sidestepped the assault, its tail knocking down small trees as it spun out of the way.

The T. rex continued to whip around, slamming its tail into the sail-back's flank. The blow sent the sail-back tumbling right toward Alan!

The scientist leaped clear just in time.

As the savage behemoths clawed and bit and battled each other, Alan spotted the rest of the group bunched together in the brush several yards away. He sprinted toward them, but was stopped by an earth-shattering crash that nearly threw him from his feet. The T. rex had fallen right into his path!

An instant later, the sail-back descended on the wounded rex. With claws flailing and maw opened wide, the giant predator latched on to the rex's throat.

Backing away in horror, Alan turned and ran to join Billy and the others.

"Come on!" Alan yelled. He led the group through the underbrush as the sail-back's triumphant bellow echoed behind him.

After reaching a safe-looking spot, Alan stopped. Grabbing the front of Paul Kirby's shirt, Alan slammed him against a tree.

"Why did you bring us here?" Alan asked. "The *truth*."

Udesky took a step forward, but Alan held him back with a look. He was tired of games. He wanted answers.

Amanda spoke up. "Our son is on this island. We need your help to find him."

Still crushed against the tree, Paul pulled a photograph from the pocket of his shorts.

"This is him," Paul said. "Eric. He's thirteen. He's just about the greatest kid in the world."

Alan let go of Paul and took the photo. It was a school-portrait-style photo of a young, dark-haired boy with bright, intelligent eyes and a fun-loving smile.

"He's with a man named Ben Hildebrand," Amanda said.

Billy raised an eyebrow in curiosity. "Who's that?"

"Her new boyfriend," Paul said sourly.

"A *friend*," Amanda said quickly. "We were vacationing. Eric wanted to see this island and the dinosaurs, so Ben found a guy who would take them parasailing. Dino-Soar. I mean, it *sounded* fun, harmless. But they never came back."

"We called everyone, did everything we could," Paul said. "No one will help us. The guy at the U.S. Embassy said we should 'accept the inevitable.' You believe that?"

"So you hired these mercenaries," Alan said.

"We prefer 'recovery specialists,'" Udesky said brusquely. "We do overseas custody issues and—"

Alan had no interest in hearing the mercenary rattle off his résumé. He interrupted the man without taking his gaze off Paul.

"You duped us into coming here," Alan said.

"We needed somebody who knew the lay of the land," Paul tried to explain. "Somebody who'd been to this island before."

Alan stared at Paul in utter disbelief. "I have *never* been to this island!"

"Sure you have," Paul said. "You wrote that book. . . ."

Billy cleared his throat. "That was Isla Nublar. This is Isla Sorna. The second island."

In a low voice, Paul said to Udesky, "I didn't know there were two islands."

Amanda moved toward Alan. "But, Dr. Grant, you survived dinosaurs before. You saved those kids."

Alan could hardly find the words to get through to these people. This was lunacy!

"A *few* of us survived," Alan said. "A lot more died. And we were better prepared and better armed."

Alan sighed heavily. He looked into Amanda's face. Then Paul's. He could see how desperate they were.

For a moment, Alan tried to put himself in their shoes. If he and Ellie had remained together, if Charlie had been *his* son, he might have gone to any lengths to save him.

"How many days have they been missing?" Alan asked.

A look passed between Amanda and Paul.

Paul straightened up. "Eight weeks."

For a moment, Alan was speechless. Then he glanced at Billy, who appeared equally stunned. *Eight weeks in this place?* thought Alan in horror. *It may as well have been eight years.*

Alan turned back to the boy's parents. Hope that their son was alive was clearly the one thing keeping them going. Unfortunately, it was keeping them going in a direction that was likely to get them all killed.

"After what you've seen today, do you really think your son could be alive?" Alan asked as gently as he could manage.

Amanda's eyes grew wide. "He's smart, Dr. Grant. And he knows so much about dinosaurs."

Before anyone else could speak, Alan put his hand out to silence them. He could not listen to any more of this.

"No," Alan said. "I'm sorry, but *no*. We'll salvage what we can from the plane. Then we head for the coast. There may be a boat left, something to get us off the island."

Paul reacted fiercely. "Dr. Grant, we're not leaving without our son."

"You can stick with us, or you can go look for him," Alan said. "Either way, you're probably not getting out of here alive."

Alan turned toward the plane, and Billy followed him.

"What do we do?" Paul asked the others.

"Well, I think we should start searching for your boy," Udesky said.

"Which way?" Paul asked.

The mercenary hesitated, then cleared his throat. "In the direction that Dr. Grant is going."

CHAPTER 5

THE FIVE SURVIVORS moved quickly and quietly through the wreckage of the plane, looking to salvage anything useful.

Billy found his camera bag, with the camera intact. Alan found a backpack. Amanda located her suitcase and went behind the plane to change into clothes better suited for the jungle.

Paul changed with her, and Amanda noticed how much trimmer her husband looked.

"How much weight have you lost?" she asked him.

"Twenty, twenty-five pounds," said Paul, clearly happy she'd noticed. "I've been swimming at the Y."

"You hate to swim," said Amanda.

"People change," said Paul meaningfully. Then he added softly, "You look good."

"So do you," said Amanda. She made brief eye contact with her husband, but then looked away.

Around the other side of the plane,

Billy had begun taking photographs of a giant footprint left in the mud by the dinosaur who had attacked the plane.

"Obviously a superpredator," said Billy.

Alan nodded, mentally running through a list of dinosaurs that would have left a similar footprint.

"Suchomimus. That snout," suggested Billy.

"They never got that big," pointed out Alan.

"Baryonyx?" asked Billy.

"Not with that sail," said Alan. "Spinosaurus aegypticus."

"I don't remember that on InGen's list," Billy said.

"That's because it wasn't on their list," Alan said. "Who knows what else they were up to?"

Alan and Billy watched Paul suspiciously as the man struggled with his backpack like an amateur.

"So, Mr. Kirby, tell me," Billy said. "When you climbed K2, did you base-camp at twenty-five or thirty thousand feet?"

"Thirty thousand, I think," Paul said. "Closer to the top."

"About a thousand feet above it, actually," Billy said as he moved closer to the man. "Most mountain climbers remember how tall the mountains were."

Paul couldn't hide his guilty expression.

"There is no Kirby Enterprises, is there?" Alan asked.

"There is," Paul said quickly. "I own a place called Kirby Paint and Tile Plus. We're out in the Westgate Shopping Center in Enid, Oklahoma."

Billy shook his head. "I don't suppose that check you wrote us is any good."

Udesky's gaze narrowed. "He paid *us* half up front. Cash."

"Mortgaged everything I had to do it," Paul said. "Even the store. And if we make it off this island with my son, I swear I'll make good on the money I owe you. I don't care if it takes me the rest of my life."

Alan and the mercenary exchanged an unhappy glance.

"However long that is," Udesky said.

As Alan led the group through the jungle, a shimmering spot of color in the trees caught his eye.

A parasail chute!

Alan allowed Udesky and Billy to climb up and investigate. They found a young adult life vest—and an adult skeleton.

"Ben," Amanda said quietly.

They found Ben's camcorder, but the footage didn't offer any clues to the mystery of what had happened to Eric—or Ben.

"Take the chute," Alan said. "We can use it to signal a plane from the coast."

Tears welled in Amanda's eyes. "No! Our baby's out there," she said. "He's out there and we've got to find him!"

She ran into the jungle. Paul and Udesky went after her.

Alan looked to Billy. "You know there's no chance. Logically, that is."

"Hey, don't go accusing me of being logical," Billy said as he finished putting the parasail into his backpack.

Alan nodded and followed the others, Billy at his side.

They found Amanda, Paul, and Udesky gathered around a large dinosaur nest. Within the nest, Alan saw twelve large eggs laid in a spiral.

He identified the species in a horrified instant.

"Raptors," Alan said.

CHAPTER 6

ALAN BLASTED THROUGH THE FOREST, the rest of his party struggling to keep up with him. He knew they could not slow down.

"What's a raptor?" Amanda asked.

"They're not that big," Udesky said. "Nothing like that thing with the sail."

"If we come across one, we *might* live," Alan said.

Paul looked relieved. "Well, that's good."

"But you never come across *just one*," Alan pointed out.

Amanda stopped suddenly. "Where's Billy?"

Studying the trees around them, Alan looked for some sign of his assistant. Raptors could take down their prey quietly and all too efficiently.

"Billy!" Alan cried automatically. "Billy!"

"I thought we weren't supposed to yell," whispered Amanda.

"Here!"

A few branches rustled and Billy appeared.

"I got some great pictures of the nest," Billy said excitedly. "This *proves* raptors raised their young in colonies! This speaks to a larger social structure—"

Alan cut him off. "This is *not* the time to have a paleontological discussion about the social patterns of raptors!"

"But I thought we might collaborate on a paper—" Billy said.

"Right, the first rule of academics," said Alan in disgust. "Publish . . . or *perish*."

Turning away in fury, Alan hoped his assistant got the message.

Hours later, the party came across the outer reaches of the vast InGen compound. No raptors had appeared. It seemed they were safe—for the moment.

The overgrown parking lot was littered with abandoned vehicles. Some lay on their sides, while others had been flipped over.

Well, Alan thought, *we're not going to be driving to the coast*.

Alan felt troubled as he looked through a partially caved-in windshield.

It looks like a giant head-butted the glass, he thought.

Alan guided the group up to the front door of an enormous building. As he approached, he thought he saw catlike movements out of the corner of his eye on the high ridge overlooking the complex. But when he looked that way, he saw nothing.

Nerves, Alan decided. *I'm jumping at shadows. At least, I hope they're just shadows.*

Inside the building, the once opulent corporate lobby was now in the process of being reclaimed by the jungle. Roots and ivy poked through the floor and walls. In the waiting room, the cushions of the sofas and chairs had been gnawed and pulled apart. Dusty coffee mugs and filled ashtrays sat on the tables.

Alan glanced at the nearby water cooler and saw that the water had turned brackish. He looked up at the sound of flapping and spotted birds nesting in the rafters. It left him with an eerie, haunted feeling.

"Eric!" Amanda called.

"Son, are you here?" Paul shouted.

Nothing.

Alan watched with interest as Amanda picked up the phone at the reception desk, but it was dead, as he expected.

"Omigosh, *food!*" Paul said as he pointed to a pair of vending machines standing at the end of the long, vine-covered hallway. Frantically, he started pulling change out of his pockets.

"Let's see," said Paul. "I've got about a dollar seventy-five. How about you guys?"

Billy watched this with a frown, then simply smashed in the windows of the two machines with his boot.

Paul sighed, glancing apologetically at Amanda. "Guess you can take the man out of civilization, but . . ." Paul's voice trailed off and he simply shrugged.

"We can eat later," Alan said after Billy handed out the candy and snacks. "We need to look for weapons and communications equipment."

"We have to make this place secure," Udesky added.

Alan and Billy led the group as they explored the rest of the building. Alan pushed through a set of doors and found himself in a cavernous hatching facility.

Much of the equipment was the same as what Alan had seen on the first island, Isla Nublar, but the sheer size of what confronted him now dwarfed the facilities on the other island.

As Alan walked down the ramp and onto the floor, he glanced at the incredible array of technology and noticed an enormous freezer whose plugs had been pulled years ago. Empty incubators and tanks of formaldehyde with dinosaur fetuses and body parts surrounded the freezer. Machines with intricate tubing and swing arms stood beside conveyor belts crisscrossing the room at different levels.

Amanda turned to Alan. "This is how you make dinosaurs?"

"This is how you play God," Alan said sourly.

Alan watched as Billy looked around the lab. He could tell the young man was impressed.

"Okay if I take pictures?" Billy asked.

Alan nodded. Amanda walked past the dinosaurs in formaldehyde and stopped.

"This tank has a sign on it," she said. "Raptors."

She peered into the eyes of the raptor head that seemed to be floating inside—then she screamed. A *live* raptor lunged at her from *behind* the tank.

The dinosaur's snapping maw was filled with a razor-sharp collection of broken, mashed, and jagged teeth. The creature's powerful three-fingered hands slashed wildly, while the retractable crescent-shaped hooks on its feet clicked and scraped at the floor.

"Aaaghhh!" Amanda cried.

The raptor's spittle splashed her face. But the predator couldn't press its body between the closely spaced tanks to reach her.

"Amanda!" Paul called.

"Back out! Move!" ordered Alan. He led the group through the lab, hoping to get them to safety before the raptor found a way between the tanks.

The group raced down the hallway, checking doors for possible escape routes or hiding places. When the raptor rounded the corner twenty feet behind them, Paul ducked into a nearby door. Alan raced inside with the others and slammed the door closed. But its lock was electrical. *Useless!*

Alan led the group down a long aisle between rows of oversized steel cages with open doors. Clearly, the cages had once been used for holding young dinosaurs, like some sort of dinosaur kennel.

Suddenly, the raptor burst into the room and leaped for the closest prey—Billy and Udesky! The pair flew into the nearest cage and slammed the door shut in the predator's angry, hissing face.

Alan, Paul, and Amanda ran to another cage. Alan grabbed the door and yanked. The loud *screech* of its rusty hinges drew the predator's attention.

Before Alan could close the door completely, the raptor slammed into it with explosive force, smashing the door past the lock and into the cage.

The group was forced up against one of the

cage's chain-link walls, trapped in a small triangle of space by the advancing door. The angry raptor clawed and hissed at them through the door. Then its head began to dart around as it searched for another way to reach its prey.

Alan followed the raptor's gaze up to the wide-open top of the small triangular space. With a shriek of triumph, the raptor's powerful form leaped at the chain-link door and started to climb.

Amanda was the fastest to react. Grabbing hold of the door, she yelled, "Push!"

Paul and Alan joined her in shoving hard against the caved-in steel door. The door scraped along the floor, hardly budging at first. Then it suddenly swung back, right through the cage's opening, with the raptor still clinging to it.

Hrrrr-reeeeee!

As the door slammed into the opposite wall, the raptor lost its grip and fell into the small space. Amanda instantly slid the door's bolt into place, trapping it there—this time the door reached up to the ceiling.

Alan knew the raptor would find a way out, but he wasn't hanging around to find out how long it would take! After racing to the end of the room, he hauled open the heavy exit door. Paul, Amanda, Billy, and Udesky were right behind him.

Hrrrr-reeeeee! cried the raptor as it fought to

free itself. The raptor growled and snarled as it launched itself against the door, but it held.

Hrrrr-reeeeee!

"That sound," Billy said.

Alan nodded. It was the same sound Billy had made with the raptor resonating chamber.

"I think he's calling for help," Alan said.

Alan led the group out the rear of the lab building and into an equipment yard. He could still hear the raptor's call as he guided the group toward the tree line.

From the jungle, the call was answered. Raptor cries quickly surrounded them. The raptors were talking to each other!

Alan couldn't believe it. His theory on raptor communication had been proven correct. Unfortunately, the proof had come at the worst possible time!

Ahead, a herd of frightened hadrosaurs responded to the raptor howls by fleeing across the equipment yard. Dozens of raptors burst from the jungle and ran after them.

"Head for the trees!" Alan yelled to the others.

Another raptor call came from behind. Alan turned to see the raptor they had trapped standing near the lab's open rear door.

Bolting ahead, Alan swiftly studied the way the raptors organized themselves. A large raptor, probably an alpha male, led the group into a hunting formation. The sight gave Alan an idea.

"This way," Alan said.

He led Billy and the others into the midst of the stampeding hadrosaur herd.

"Stay together!" Alan called. "Stay—"

It was useless. In seconds, the group was split up in the chaos. Alan looked back again.

His plan had failed. The raptors were ignoring the hadrosaurs. They were only interested in the humans.

This makes no sense, Alan thought. *If all they want is fresh food, why not attack the hadrosaurs?*

As Alan darted to escape being run down by the crazed hadrosaurs, he saw Billy fall. He gasped. Had a raptor pulled Billy down? Trying not to panic, Alan moved through the blurred mass of dinosaurs. He found Billy's camera bag and snatched it up. The strap had either broken on its own—or been cut by a razor-sharp raptor claw.

Then Alan heard voices from the other side of the stampede. He glimpsed Billy, Paul, Amanda, and Udesky gathered together. A line of raptors was racing their way!

"Alan!" called Billy.

"Keep going!" yelled Alan, knowing they had no choice but to separate.

CHAPTER 7

DR. ALAN GRANT WAS NOW crouched in a network of heavy branches. The sun was beginning to set. Soon it would be evening.

Below him, a pack of angry raptors waited. At the moment, he remained just beyond their reach, but they weren't giving up their watch.

As terrified as he was, Alan couldn't help but be fascinated by their communication. Their chirps and barks were like a nightmarish birdsong. It had a rhythm. A structure. Just like speech.

They kept "saying" the same thing, over and over. Under his breath, he mimicked the raptors' speech patterns.

What does that mean? he wondered as he looked into the dark eyes of the predators. *What are you saying?*

The predators' only reply was the same series of chirps and barks. Then one of the raptors jumped higher and nearly caught his foot.

Alan looked up. He wanted to climb

higher, but he couldn't see any branches that would support his weight.

Suddenly, he heard a low creaking. A *crack.*

The branch he stood upon was starting to give!

Trying to control his fear, he looked down at the faces of the predators. He was about to become their next meal. . . .

Crick-crack. Snap. Hssssssss.

A small canister suddenly landed at the base of the tree, spraying out a thick cloud of oily fog! Four more canisters landed near the raptors and spewed more of the caustic mist.

The raptors recoiled and screamed in pain. Shrieking, they ran off blindly.

Alan's eyes burned from the gas. He saw a human shape moving through the fog below.

"Come on! They'll be back!" called a voice.

Alan half climbed and half fell out of the tree. A small, dirty hand reached out and grabbed his arm. He stumbled and coughed as he rushed to get through the thickest part of the smoke cloud.

Several minutes later, Alan's blurred vision began to clear. He was deeper in the jungle and he could no longer hear the raptors. The mysterious figure led him into a rocky stream.

In the golden glow of twilight, he looked down at the face of his rescuer. The boy removed the rag that had encircled his nose and mouth. At first, all

Alan could see was the filth and grime covering the boy's flesh and the camouflage cloak of leaves that draped his torn clothes. Then the boy removed the safety goggles he'd been wearing, and Alan saw the boy's eyes.

They were bright and intelligent. The same eyes he had seen in a photograph from Paul Kirby's wallet.

These were Eric Kirby's eyes.

Only—there was something different about the look in them now. Something *wild*.

He almost didn't seem human.

CHAPTER 8

ERIC LED THE WAY along the stream. The man he'd rescued was uncoordinated, and the way he tramped along the ground was *loud*. Eric was worried the predators would hear them.

Finally, they came to a swampy pond where a rusting tanker truck sat headlight-deep in the water. Eric opened the tanker's hatch and crawled through. The tall man followed, and the hatch closed with an iron clang. Then Eric sealed it shut behind them and lit a small, battery-powered lantern.

The man settled into Eric's living space, which was no bigger than the inside of a van.

"Thanks a lot, Eric—" said the man.

Eric held up his hand. He listened for a moment, his ears attuned to the familiar sounds of lurking predators. Then he turned his gaze back on the man.

"You know who I am?" asked Eric.

"Yes. Your parents are both here," said

the man. "They're looking for you."

"On the island?" Eric asked. *Together?*

Alan nodded. "Yes. Together."

Eric stared. He couldn't believe it. He had been hoping to be rescued, but by his parents?

His shoulders slumped.

"They'll never make it," he said quietly. "I mean, they can't even manage when the cable goes out. And . . . they don't do so well together."

"You'd be surprised what people can do when they have to," the man said.

Eric wanted to believe that. He looked at the man again. The face seemed familiar. After seeing no other living beings except dinosaurs for so long, Eric had almost started to think of himself as one of the animals loose on the island. His memory of other human beings, of their faces, their voices, had been fading.

Eric switched on a second lantern and the dim glow of light in the van brightened. He looked again at the man's face, and a jolt of recognition hit him.

"You're Alan Grant!" Eric said.

Dr. Grant looked surprised to be recognized.

"I read both of your books," Eric told him.

"And which one did you prefer?"

"The first one," Eric said. "Before you were on the island. You liked dinosaurs back then."

"Well," Dr. Grant said with a slightly bitter laugh, "back *then,* they hadn't tried to *eat* me."

"What are *you* doing here?"

"Your parents—they invited me to come with them . . . to look for you."

Eric watched the scientist look at his hide-away. He seemed impressed. Eric had scavenged a great deal. There were some battery-powered lanterns, a pair of binoculars, and lots of candy wrappers. Eric had been living mostly on chocolate and other junk food for weeks.

"When InGen cleared out, they left a lot of stuff behind," Eric said.

"Any weapons, radios?" Dr. Grant asked.

"I used the last of the gas grenades just now," said Eric.

"And I appreciate it," Dr. Grant said; then he looked around the space again. Against a wall he saw a bottle half filled with a murky yellow liquid. He picked it up.

"Don't open that!" said Eric quickly.

"Why not?"

"It came from a T. rex. Keeps some of the smaller ones away, but it seems to attract another really big one with a sail."

Dr. Grant carefully put the bottle down again. "Anything else you used as a . . . ah . . . weapon?"

Eric pulled out a long cattle prod. "Found this,

but the battery's dead."

"It's a wonder you aren't," Dr. Grant said, shaking his head in disbelief. "I'm astonished, Eric. I barely lasted thirty hours. You've lasted eight weeks."

Eric shuddered. *"Eight weeks.* Is that all it's been?" He had honestly thought it had been much longer.

"The important thing is we both made it," said Dr. Grant reassuringly. "That's something we have in common."

Eric shrugged.

"Did you read Malcolm's book?" asked Dr. Grant.

"Yeah," said Eric.

Ian Malcolm was a rival scientist. Like Dr. Grant, he had been trapped on Jurassic Park once, too.

"What did you think?" asked Dr. Grant.

"I dunno. I mean, it was kind of preachy. Chaos this, chaos that. And like, to me, the guy seemed kind of high on himself."

Dr. Grant smiled. "That's *two* things we have in common."

Eric found it difficult to listen any longer. He was tired and hungry. Reaching into his pocket, he withdrew the candy bar he had scavenged just before he spotted Dr. Grant and the raptors. He'd learned the hard way not to keep too much food in his shelter.

He was halfway finished with the candy bar before he noticed the hard swallows of his companion.

Oh, right, Eric reminded himself. *Humans share food.*

"Here," Eric said. He handed the other half of the bar to Dr. Grant, then watched with fascination as the otherwise reserved scientist tore into it like a Tyrannosaurus rex he'd seen savaging its prey.

A few miles away, Eric's parents were still worried sick about him. Perched with Billy up in the tree-tops, they were far from safe. Sadly, they had lost Udesky to the raptors, but nothing had come after them for a while, so they settled in for the night. At daybreak, they would resume the search for their son—and Alan.

Seeing his wife crying, Paul turned toward her. "I just want you to know, Amanda, it's not your fault what happened."

Amanda sniffed, clearly miserable.

"Eric has always been headstrong," continued Paul, "and you throw Ben Hildebrand into the mix, and, well . . ."

"Well what?"

"Well water. I don't want to speak ill of the dead. What I'm trying to say is, it was just a crazy accident. The exact same thing could have happened if he was with me."

Amanda shook her head. "This wouldn't have happened if he was with *you*." Her voice sounded so sad, so full of regret—not just about their son, but also about their marriage. "I mean, you drive five miles an hour below the speed limit. I totaled three cars in five years—"

"Well . . . the Buick wasn't really totaled," Paul admitted. "I just said it was. I . . . I wanted to get the SUV."

"He would have been safe with you, Paul," Amanda insisted. "But I wanted him to see more of the world than Enid, Oklahoma. And *I* wanted to see more of the world than Enid, Oklahoma. And so, yes, it's my fault this happened. I'm sorry that you have to be here."

Paul's answer was simple: "I'm not sorry at all."

Tears staining her cheeks, Amanda met her husband's gaze. She wasn't just grateful for Paul's answer. For the first time in years, she was simply grateful for Paul.

CHAPTER 9

MORNING BROUGHT A LOW MIST to the forest floor of Isla Sorna, and Eric sealed up his hideaway for what he hoped would be the last time. As he and Alan left the truck, Eric took one of his prized possessions from his pocket and showed it to the scientist.

"Know what this is?" Eric asked.

Alan examined the sharp-edged, three-inch-long sickle-shaped object. "A raptor claw. I used to have one. A fossil."

Eric grinned, remembering exactly how he had gained this prize. "Mine's *new*."

Alan looked at him strangely and handed back the claw as if he were placing his fingers near the mouth of a very dangerous animal. Eric took in the scientist's discomfort and felt ashamed of the feral pride he'd shown only a moment before.

It's going to be all right, Eric told himself. He had to force himself to evolve from the wild survivor he had become into a human being once more. He *had* to. It would break his heart to have his mom or dad look at him the way Dr. Grant just had.

"How much of the island have you explored?" Alan asked.

"I stayed close to the compound," Eric said, though that wasn't *entirely* true. There had been more than one time when he'd been forced to stray pretty far from the complex. But if he told Dr. Grant any of *those* stories, the man might never look at him like a regular thirteen-year-old again.

"I figured if anyone came to look for me, that's where they'd start," said Eric.

"We need to head for the coast," Alan said.

Eric stopped. "What about my mom and dad?"

"They went through the compound already, and they didn't find you," Alan said. "The coast is where they'll be heading next."

"Are you sure?" Eric pressed.

"Why?" asked Alan.

"Closer you get to the water," Eric noted, "the bigger things get."

Eric and Alan walked in silence after that. Dinosaurs might be anywhere, so it was imporant to move quietly.

When they came to a clearing, they discovered

a ridge that looked over a distant river far below. The river was half shrouded in fog. Alan used the binoculars.

"There's a derelict barge resting against the riverbank. It looks to be in good shape," Alan said.

He handed the binoculars to Eric, who tried to spot the barge.

"A rescue boat?" Eric asked.

"No, something left behind. But it floats." Alan searched the canyon. "All we need to do is find a way down. Then we could follow the river out to the ocean."

Eric opened his mouth to speak.

Alan cut him off with a gesture. "We'll keep looking for your parents along the way. With any luck, the Costa Rican Coast Guard will pick us all up."

"Then we go home?" Eric asked.

Alan nodded. "Then we go home."

Suddenly, a familiar ringing sounded nearby. Eric instantly recognized the distinct and annoying melody.

"That sounds like my dad's phone!" Eric said. He rushed off to follow the sound. Alan tried to slow him down, but Eric was too fast for him.

"Wait!" Alan called. "How do you know?"

Eric sang to the electronic jingle. "Kirby Paint

and Tile Plus—in Westgate!" The ringing grew louder. "Dad? *DAD?*"

In an instant, Eric was no longer a wild boy, focused every waking moment on survival. Suddenly, he was the kid from Enid, Oklahoma, again—and he was desperate for his parents to take him home and keep him safe. Reaching them was all that mattered.

Eric raced ahead. The phone stopped ringing, but he heard other sounds now. Human voices. People calling his name.

"Mom! Dad!" Eric yelled.

He burst into a meadow and saw them shouting, "Eric!"

As he ran to meet them, he read their features—disbelief, joy, terror, relief, love. Every emotion seemed to be there in his parents' faces. It had been so long since he'd seen human emotions, it felt wonderful!

The only thing standing between Eric and his parents now was one of InGen's giant dinosaur fences. Eric ran up to it, his fingers curling around the metal bars. He looked up and saw that it could not be climbed over. There was a line of rusty spikes on the top.

Paul and Amanda hugged their son through the fence.

Amanda managed a kiss, too.

"Sweetheart," she said, almost out of breath. "You're okay. You're okay!"

Eric's dad squared his shoulders proudly. "Never had a doubt. Never did. Us Kirby men, we stick around, huh?"

"We do," Eric said.

Eric's mom licked her shirttail and tried to rub his face clean through the fence. Eric used to hate it when she did that. Now he didn't even think of pulling away. He just smiled and let her scrub.

"Honey," Paul said, touching Amanda's shoulder, "there's not enough spit in the world for that."

Amanda laughed. It sounded to Eric as if it had been the first time she'd laughed in months.

Billy caught up with the Kirbys at the same time Alan reached Eric.

Alan looked unhappily at the fence standing between them. "We need to find a gap."

Everyone walked along the fence, looking for an opening.

Eric stayed close to his parents.

"So, sport," his dad asked, "how did you know we were so close?"

"I heard your phone ring," Eric said. "That stupid jingle from the store."

"My phone?" his dad asked. His forehead creased and he frowned in confusion. He searched his pockets and backpack as the others watched.

"Where is it?" Amanda asked.

"I don't know," Paul said. "I didn't think I had it with me."

"When did you use it last?" Amanda asked.

Paul shrugged. "I don't remember."

"Think," Amanda said. Her brief calm was fading.

Paul shook his head. "The plane. I got a call on the plane, put the phone in my coat pocket, and—"

Paul's gentle expression changed, tensing with an awful realization.

"What?" Amanda demanded. "WHAT?"

"I loaned it to Nash," Paul said quietly. "He must have had it on him when he . . ."

Eric looked to his parents, Billy, and Alan. They all appeared horror-struck.

"I don't understand," Eric said. "Who's Nash?"

The ringing came again, accompanied by heavy footfalls. Something *big* was coming.

"When the plane was attacked," Alan said. "Nash was—"

Eric heard a growl and the sound of a small tree falling. He saw a huge dinosaur appear on his side of the fence and stand motionless at the edge of the jungle. It was over sixteen feet high, nearly fifty feet long, and had a crocodile-shaped head and a mouth full of long, sharp teeth. Along its back, a five-foot-tall sail glistened in the dappled sunlight.

Spinosaurus, realized Eric instantly. And this guy Nash had obviously become spino breakfast.

The dinosaur's jaws parted. *Rahhhhrrrr-grahhhrrrr!*

"Run," Alan said in not much more than a whisper.

Alan and Eric bolted as the Spinosaurus came crashing out of the trees. Amanda, Paul, and Billy kept up with them on the other side of the fence.

Alan pointed at a small hole in the fence, which had probably been made by one of the smaller dinosaurs.

"Through there!" Alan yelled.

Eric dove through the opening. He rolled and came to his feet. Turning, he saw Alan following. The Spinosaurus was a foot behind him, its jaws about to close on Alan's legs, when the scientist hauled himself through to safety!

SNAP!

The Spinosaurus's mouth closed in frustration and the animal roared as it flung itself at the fence, clawing and tearing with savage fury!

Everyone ran toward a concrete building at the edge of the canyon. Eric glanced back to see the Spinosaurus crashing through the fence. It was coming after them!

When they reached the building, Alan hauled the steel doors open and the others rushed inside. The dinosaur's thunderous footfalls grew louder as Alan slammed the steel doors shut. The doors were clearly designed to be secure, with heavy bolts on the top and bottom. Alan slid the last bolt as the Spinosaurus smashed against the far side.

Eric gasped. The hinges strained but held. The dinosaur struck again and again, then scraped its claws against the door. Finally, it stopped. There was no way the dinosaur was getting in.

Eric heard his parents sigh. Then they threw their arms around him.

Taking a deep breath, he returned their hug.

He never wanted to let them go.

A few feet away from Eric's reunion with his parents, Alan took a look around. They were in a single room with giant windows designed to look into the canyon beyond.

Looks like an observatory of some sort, thought Alan, *but to observe what?*

He tried looking out one of the windows, but a thick fog obscured his view.

He saw Billy approach him.

"Udesky?" Alan asked. "Where is he?"

"Raptors got him," Billy said, shaking his head.

"They set a trap. Can you believe it? They wounded him. Tried to get us to help. We almost did, and then they sprang at us. We ran, went up the trees, but Udesky didn't make it."

Alan listened grimly. "We'll get out of this. We just need to keep moving."

Alan started for the center of the room, where a staircase spiraled downward.

"Hold on," Billy said, grabbing his mentor's arm. "I want to tell you that I'm so sorry. I could have gotten you killed. I know that. It was stupid."

Alan just stared at his student.

A few feet away, Paul, Amanda, and Eric heard the strain in Billy's voice and turned to listen.

"Please, just yell at me. Call me an idiot. I know I screwed up," continued Billy.

Alan's gaze narrowed. He had no idea what his student was talking about—and he had a feeling he didn't *want* to know.

Lowering his head, Billy said in a conspiratorial whisper, "What did you do with them?"

"With *what*?" asked Alan. "Billy, what are you talking about?"

Billy finally seemed to realize that Alan wasn't following. He didn't *know*. He hadn't looked in the camera bag!

"In my bag," Billy said.

Alan opened Billy's camera bag to find a pair of raptor eggs! Both were intact. He'd been carrying them all this time.

"I just thought if we got a raptor egg back to the mainland, we could study it in a controlled environment," Billy quickly explained.

Alan stared at his assistant, unable to accept what Billy had done. Those raptors had stalked him relentlessly for one reason—they'd wanted their eggs!

Billy spoke even more quickly. "Plus it would be easy to get money. Enough to fund the digging for ten years. More. Whatever it took."

Disgusted, Alan shook his head.

"I did it with the best of intentions," Billy pleaded.

"Some of the worst things imaginable have been done with the *best* of intentions," Alan said. "You rushed in with no thought of the consequences, to yourself or anyone else."

Billy stared speechlessly, stung by the force of Alan's anger.

"You're no better than the people who built this place," concluded Alan. Then he turned away, leaving Billy to consider his words.

CHAPTER 10

ALAN STOOD NEAR THE STAIRS at the center of the room, still stunned by what he had just learned.

Paul approached him. "What do you think this place is?"

"Some kind of observatory," answered Alan. "It looks over the canyon."

Eric nodded. "We saw a boat at the bottom. Just downriver. We can get off the island."

"Come on," Alan said. He headed down the spiral staircase, leaving Billy with his guilt. Paul and the others fell in line after Alan. Eventually, Billy followed—at a distance.

The rusty stairs stopped on a lower level below the observation room. Above and around them, the fog was thick; yet below them, the view was clear enough for Alan to make out the river and the barge he and Eric had spotted earlier from the canyon ridge.

Alan held Billy's camera bag over the edge, ready to drop it into the canyon. But Paul stopped him, hand raised.

"Can I offer a suggestion?" Paul asked. "Keep the eggs with you. At least until we get off the island."

Eric shook his head. "But then the raptors might keep following us, looking for the eggs!"

Paul smiled. "And maybe they'll follow us anyway, just for taking them. I've been working in sales my whole life, and if there's one thing I've learned, it's that if you've got something the other fella wants, you don't give it up. Those things may want us dead, but they want those eggs more. That's the only advantage we've got."

Alan looked at him closely. Paul Kirby was more than a panicked father. More than a bumbling liar. There was something about this man, something he hadn't seen before.

Alan removed his pack and put the camera case back inside. Shouldering the pack, he led the way down the ramp to the landing, where a set of rusty stairs continued down the canyon wall.

Alan had taken only a few steps down when the crumbling staircase broke away! Paul grabbed Alan's arm and pulled him up as the staircase fell. It clanged against the canyon wall, then crashed far below.

"You okay?" Paul asked.

Alan nodded shakily and looked toward their only alternative now, a fragile-looking catwalk that extended out from the landing where they stood.

"How about this way?" proposed Alan. "There's probably another stairway on the other side."

"Do you think it goes all the way across?" Eric asked. The fog was so thick around them, they couldn't even see where the catwalk ended.

"One way to find out," Alan said. He had not fully recovered from his near fall, but he knew the only way to get over it was to push on. Even so, his stomach turned at being up so high.

Alan started across the catwalk, with Amanda close behind. Under their combined weight, the catwalk groaned unsteadily. Alan glanced back at Amanda, who had frozen with fear.

"We'd better do this *one* at a time," Alan said.

Amanda nodded quickly and stepped off the catwalk.

Alan carefully moved forward. The thick fog closed in behind him, cutting off his view of the group—and their view of him.

All they could rely on was the slow creaking sound of the catwalk as he moved across it.

After a few minutes, Alan stopped. He'd reached a lateral support beam that provided a small landing where he could catch his breath.

Out of the dead silence, he heard an uncertain voice from the fog. "Dr. Grant?"

It was Paul. He sounded nervous, as if he wasn't sure he'd get an answer.

"It's okay! Come on over," Alan called. "One at a time."

At the far side of the catwalk, Amanda stepped forward gingerly. She turned back to Eric.

"Eric, it's okay," she said. "Mommy's got to leave you for just a minute, but you'll be right behind. . . ."

"Mom, I've survived alone on this island for eight weeks," Eric said flatly. "I think I can handle the next two minutes without you."

Paul and Amanda exchanged a look. Their "baby" was no longer a baby.

Eric shot his mother a smile. She nodded and moved ahead, into the mist.

They were all in this together now, that was for sure.

While he waited for the others to reach the landing, Alan tried to get a sense of where he was and what purpose this place may have served. High arched walls of steel mesh were braced by support beams. It looked as if they were all inside a vast cage. But *what* was the cage designed to hold?

The catwalk creaked loudly as someone approached through the dense fog. Amanda appeared.

"That was fun," she said, gasping and rolling her eyes.

"Wasn't it, though?" Alan said.

She turned and called, "Okay! Come on, Eric!"

Alan moved across the lateral support to make room for the others. When his hand touched the railing, he sent a white, hardened substance dropping into the mist. Looking up, he noticed a large strut covered with the same substance.

"Oh, no," Alan whispered. He suddenly had a very good idea of what the white substance was—and what this place had been designed to hold.

"What is it?" Amanda asked.

"This place," Alan said. "It's a birdcage."

Amanda's eyes widened with fear. "For what?"

"Something else InGen didn't put on the list," Alan said.

Then they both heard Eric's cries.

"We're not alone!" Eric yelled, trying to warn the others.

He backed up slowly on the catwalk as a looming shape emerged from the fog. A full-grown Pteranodon approached. It was over seven feet tall and walked upright on clawed feet. The reptile's forty-five-foot wings were folded batlike at its sides.

The cone-shaped orange-and-black-striped crest jutting from the back of the gray-winged reptile's skull clearly marked it as a Pteranodon, but according to paleontologists, Pteranodons weren't supposed to have wingspans this large. This creature was a genetically engineered *giant*!

The way its weight made the bridge shift and sway also made Eric think that it was *a lot* heavier than the fifty to eighty pounds a Pteranodon was supposed to weigh. That meant it could be stronger than the Pteranodons who sailed the sky 65 million years ago, during the Age of Dinosaurs—stronger and capable of practically anything. A true Pteranodon couldn't lift a boy his size. But *this* creature . . .

The Pteranodon fixed Eric with a terrifying stare.

It was far from the first time over the past eight weeks that Eric had looked into such dark, hungry eyes.

You wanna eat me? an angry Eric challenged silently. *Then catch me!*

He turned and dashed back along the teetering catwalk. The Pteranodon spread its wings and glided directly toward him.

Eric ran toward his father and Billy. But just before Eric reached them, the Pteranodon swooped out of the fog and snatched him off the catwalk. He gasped, then screamed as he was carried into the air.

This was one game of tag he'd just lost.

Eric was carried by the Pteranodon deep into the canyon. They swooped over an isolated outcropping of rocks.

Then, with a sudden cry, the Pteranodon let Eric fall into the mist below!

CHAPTER 11

WITH A JARRING THUMP, Eric landed in what looked like a large bowl of mud and branches the size of a giant satellite dish. Something crackled and crunched beneath him. He looked down and saw that he was sitting on a pile of dinosaur bones, picked clean.

Then a human skull rolled into his lap.

Horrified, Eric was about to scream when he heard a sharp cry above him.

Caahhhhhrrr!

Eric looked up to see six Pteranodon hatchlings closing in on him with their sharp-edged beaks.

Eric knew he'd just become this Pteranodon family's version of fast food— a snack picked up for the kiddies. A human Happy Meal!

But Eric wasn't about to give up. He'd learned the hard way how to make the most out of the least bit around him.

Taking the human skull in one hand

and a heavy dinosaur thighbone in the other, Eric brandished his makeshift weapons as the hungry hatchlings chittered and screeched and came at him.

Paul reached the canyon wall, turned a corner, and ran along a second enclosed catwalk leading deeper into the canyon.

Amanda and Alan came pounding down the catwalk, trying to keep up.

"Where is he?" Amanda shouted to Paul. "Can you see him?"

Paul turned and shouted back. "I'm trying! That thing took him down this way!"

Alan heard a sound far above. He looked up to see Billy leaning out one of the huge observation deck windows. He felt a sudden chill as he guessed what Billy was about to do.

"Billy, wait!" Alan yelled.

His assistant looked back. "It's okay. I know the consequences."

Alan watched helplessly as Billy leaped from the ledge—and plunged into the canyon below. Billy fell past Alan and the Kirbys, plummeting like a stone toward certain death.

Then a colorful wing suddenly unfurled above him—it was the Dino-Soar parasail he'd retrieved from Eric and Ben's crash site!

Billy caught an updraft and started to rise.

With a look of fierce determination, Billy swooped dangerously close to the canyon wall, then headed in the direction in which Eric had been taken.

Eric was covered in sweat. The adrenaline that had kept him going this long was beginning to fade.

Swinging the bone like a sword and using the skull as a shield, Eric smacked the beak of a hatchling that had almost gotten close enough to bite his arm. Only a minute ago, that wouldn't have happened. He was getting tired. Running out of juice.

The hatchlings seemed to sense his weariness. They redoubled their attack, forcing Eric to one side of the nest. He risked a glance over the edge and saw only a huge drop.

No way out, he thought.

A blur of motion came from the sky. Eric tensed, worried that the hatchling's mother was returning.

Chancing a look up, he cried out with joy at the sight of Billy swooping overhead, using the parasail chute to fly. But Billy was too high to reach him!

"Eric! Hold on!" called Billy.

Eric hefted the skull and bone as the hatchlings moved closer—and attacked again!

Paul rounded a corner and finally caught sight of Eric in the nest, a hundred feet away. His son was fighting the hatchlings.

"Hang on, Eric!" Paul shouted. He doubted his son could hear him.

The catwalk led to a rocky area near Eric. But just ahead, there was a break where a section had fallen out. It was a jump of at least twelve feet. Paul didn't know if he could make it.

Paul heard Amanda and Alan coming up behind him and ignored their calls. He cast aside his fear, steeling himself for the jump.

He drew a deep breath.

And hesitated.

His hesitation cost him. Suddenly, a second Pteranodon crash-landed on the catwalk's enclosure above them, right next to a gaping hole in the mesh. The catwalk groaned with the extra weight.

The Pteranodon jammed its head through the hole, snapping at them.

Alan, Paul, and Amanda turned to head the other way. The Pteranodon lifted into the air and came down in front of them, lunging through another hole in the mesh, blocking their escape.

All along the cliff face, the metal catwalk supports groaned with the strain. Joints creaked, and sections of the catwalk began to sway.

Eric kicked and swung at the hatchlings. He wouldn't be able to fight them off much longer!

With a *whoosh*, Billy finally swooped down.

Eric dropped the skull and bone and jumped as high as he could. He reached Billy's boot and grabbed on with both hands. Blinding pain shot through his arms and shoulders as he was violently yanked upward, but he wouldn't let go.

The winding river and the canyon walls blurred as Billy and Eric sailed away from the nest.

Suddenly, the giant mother Pteranodon spotted them. It raced forward and tore a piece out of the parasail with its beak.

Eric and Billy began to drop!

Alan warily eyed the Pteranodon that had landed on top of the catwalk. It snapped at them through the hole in the enclosure, unfurled its great wings, and stamped on the roof.

Alan gripped the rail to steady himself as the catwalk swayed and bounced. Amanda and Paul did the same.

The mesh above suddenly gave way and the

Pteranodon slammed through and landed on the catwalk. Alan and the Kirbys were trapped inside the enclosed catwalk with the enraged Pteranodon!

The reptile came lurching their way, flailing its leathery wings and screeching in anger. Alan and the Kirbys ran for their lives along the creaking catwalk. The group rounded a corner, only to find a broken section of catwalk had fallen away into the river.

They were trapped inside the steel enclosure with nowhere to run!

As if it sensed their fear, the Pteranodon advanced. The catwalk groaned and tilted alarmingly.

Suddenly, their section of the catwalk detached from the wall and flipped over. Alan and the Kirbys fell and were caught by the mesh that had been the ceiling only moments before.

Cahhhrrrr!

The Pteranodon held on to what was now the underside of the catwalk. It flapped its wings wildly as it changed its grip on the swaying structure; then it inched toward Alan, Paul, and Amanda like a hungry spider.

Eric and Billy sailed low over the river as the Pteranodon circled them.

"Let go!" Billy yelled to Eric. "It's the only way."

Eric looked down at the choppy water and released his grip. With a great splash, he dropped into the cold river.

Surfacing quickly, he swam frantically toward shore, knowing he was far from safe. He remembered that Pteranodons hunted low over the water, snatching their prey from the surface.

Fearfully glancing over his shoulder, Eric didn't see any Pteranodons coming for him. But he did catch sight of Billy. He was trying to rise high into the air again, but the parasail's rigging was too badly damaged.

In horror, Eric watched as his rescuer flew right into the canyon wall!

Billy's harness became caught on a rock spire above him. Now he was trapped, hanging without any cover, right in the middle of Pteranodon territory!

Up on the catwalk, Alan, Paul, and Amanda watched in terror as the Pteranodon moved toward them. With an agonizing screech of metal, the far end of the catwalk gave way. It detached from the canyon wall and swung downward!

In a tangle of arms, legs, and wings, they were

all sent plummeting off the metal frame toward the river below. They quickly became untangled and the Pteranodon took flight as the humans plunged into the water.

Alan hit the water so hard the wind was knocked out of him. It took him nearly a minute to struggle to the surface, where he took in great gulps of air and spotted Amanda and Paul surfacing nearby.

The current dragged all three downstream.

From the shore, Eric watched as Billy frantically attempted to unhook the harness. Two Pteranodons landed near Billy and eyed him with delight—and hunger.

Cut it, Eric thought. *You've got to find something sharp and cut it!*

Cries from downstream drew Eric's attention. Several yards away from where the mesh of the aviary met the river, Eric saw his parents emerge from the water and race toward him. Eric allowed his mother to take him into her arms while his father pointed ahead.

"Look!" Paul said.

There was a paved road on the shore and a double-gated portal designed to allow trucks to enter and exit the area safely. Eric and his mother raced to the portal and pushed on the corroded latch, trying to open the rusted gates.

At the same time, Alan waded to shore and scanned the canyon, searching for Billy. It didn't take him long to spot his student.

Above, as Billy struggled with the harness, a huge Pteranodon lunged at him. He dodged as best he could—and the Pteranodon's bite severed part of the harness!

Billy wriggled free and dropped into the water.

Eric and his parents were pushing the second gate open when they heard Billy's cry. They turned and watched as Billy hit the water and sank—then quickly bobbed to the surface!

"He made it!" shouted Alan with relief.

Billy looked their way as a flock of Pteranodons circled above.

Alan was overjoyed to see Billy swimming toward him, safe and sound. But as Billy waded to shore, Alan's smile quickly faded. The entire flock of Pteranodons was diving down from above in pursuit of their lost prey.

"Billy, look out!" Alan yelled.

Billy glanced behind him. Then he raced forward, motioning for his companions to turn and run.

"Get back!" Billy called. "Get back!"

The giant Pteranodon's beak struck Billy with a calculated and brutal blow. Billy stumbled and fell to the ground.

Alan rushed forward, with Paul right after him.

Billy screamed as the entire flock of Pteranodons swarmed around him, picking at him with their beaks and claws.

"Billy!" Alan shouted.

He was about to race forward, but Paul held him back.

"It's no use, Dr. Grant. No use. They'll just attack you, too."

Suddenly, three of the Pteranodons broke away from Billy and headed toward the other humans.

As difficult as it was to leave Billy behind, Alan and Paul made a run for it. They raced for the birdcage's double-gated portal, where Eric and Amanda had just escaped, but the Pteranodons were too close. Alan knew they could never make it through the gates in time.

Just as the reptiles were about to swoop in for the kill, Alan and Paul dove back into the freezing water of the river.

Taking deep breaths, Alan and Paul dove down

just as the terrible beak of the lead Pteranodon knifed toward them.

Alan's lungs burned as he swam under the mesh line with Paul. When he resurfaced on the other side of the birdcage, he began gasping for air.

Suddenly, the mammoth Pteranodons crashed into the mesh behind them, screaming in rage through the bars.

"Over there!" Paul yelled. He and Alan swam to the dock up ahead. Amanda and Eric were already on the rusty barge.

Alan and Paul climbed on board; then Amanda and Eric pushed them away from the dock.

As the current drew them downstream, Eric took his first look at the incredible aviary and gasped with awe. It was a vast domed mesh structure that spanned the entire canyon. Eric saw the others catch their breath as they looked at the cage from which all but one of them had just escaped.

Shaking his head, Alan clenched his fists in anger.

What kind of mind would try to put Pteranodons in a birdcage?! Alan railed to himself. It was hubris, pure hubris. Pride so excessive that it failed to see the recklessness of its acts. And because of that recklessness, he had lost his apprentice and friend.

"Good-bye, Billy," Alan whispered, sadly looking to the horizon.

"Good-bye, Billy," Eric echoed beside Alan. "Thank you."

Turning, Eric saw Alan looking his way, his eyes wide as if something were only now occurring to him.

Then the scientist quickly turned away. He heard the angry cries of the flying reptiles echoing off the canyon walls.

The giant Pteranodon who had been cheated of the prize she had taken to feed her young stood on the shore, staring at the iron gate.

She stalked toward it slowly, some instinct telling her that this familiar section of her world had changed in some small but vital way.

She nudged at the gate and heard a sharp, tinny sound that startled her. With an angry caw, she leaped back, her wings striking the gates as she fought to keep from falling.

Then she saw it. The gate hung an inch ajar. The shiny bar the prey had used to secure it in place was dangling helplessly.

She pushed at the gate and it moved.

Again.

Again.

The door opened—and the predator stepped through, into an unsuspecting world.

The food would be hers again.

No one was going to cheat her hatchlings.

No one.

CHAPTER 12

"MY OWN KID WAS right in front of me, and I didn't do a thing," said Paul angrily after starting the barge's engine.

Amanda stood beside her husband at the stern, bailing water with a rusted bucket.

"You couldn't have made that jump," insisted Amanda.

"I should have tried. It should have been *me* on that beach back there, not Billy."

"How would that have helped Eric?" asked Amanda. "He needs you, Paul. He needs *us*."

"He could have died."

"But he didn't. And neither did you. . . . I'm sorry about Billy, Paul. I really am. But I'm *glad* you and Eric are alive."

"Check it out," Eric said to Alan at the bow after spying on his parents at the stern. "They almost look like they're getting along."

Alan grunted uncomfortably and turned away. Eric knew Alan was still thinking about Billy. And maybe something else . . .

"I'm sorry about Billy," Eric said. "He saved my life."

"You're no better than the people who made this place," Alan said softly.

"What?"

"That was the last thing I said to Billy," explained Alan. "'You're no better than the people who made this place.'"

"Do you have any kids?" Eric asked.

"No," said Alan. "Although I've studied them in the wild."

Eric's brow furrowed. He wasn't *quite* sure how to take that.

Alan shrugged. "I have a theory that there's two kinds of boys. Those who want to be astronomers and those who want to be astronauts."

Eric nodded. "I want to be an astronaut."

Alan waved his hands awkwardly. "See, *I* was just the opposite. I never understood why anyone would want to go into space. It's so *dangerous*. In space, you do *one* thing wrong and you're dead. The astronomer—or the paleontologist—gets to study these amazing things from a place of complete safety."

"Uh-huh," Eric said.

One of the ways Eric had kept himself alive on the island was by figuring out what was on a dinosaur's mind just by reading its body language.

Now Eric tried to do the same with Alan. As Alan talked, Eric studied the man's hands, his eyes, his posture, and knew at once that Dr. Grant wasn't trying to convince *him* of anything. The man was trying to convince *himself*!

Alan's eyes lit up. "You see, then? Everything you really need to learn you can learn from the ground."

Eric's piercing gaze held the man. "But then you never get to go into space."

"Exactly," Alan said. "The difference between imagining and seeing. To be able to touch them. That's what Billy wanted to do."

It was at that moment the barge rounded a bend in the river and an incredible sight came into view.

"Dr. Grant—" Eric whispered.

The crimson sun was setting over a verdant valley filled with dinosaurs. Eric could see armored ankylosaurs with massive clubbed tails and duck-billed corythosaurs. The barge lazily floated under the gigantic, arching necks of fifty-foot brachiosaurs.

With the drifting mist from the river, and the play of waning light on the lush vegetation, the scene looked like a primal Eden.

Eric looked over to Alan. For a few long moments, the paleontologist appeared mesmerized by the beauty and wonder of the island.

"I can blame the people who made this island," Alan finally said softly. "But I can't blame the people who want to see it. To study it." He gazed down at Eric. "After all, how's a boy supposed to resist this?"

Eric nodded. He couldn't have agreed more.

That night, as the barge floated farther downstream, the full moon passed behind the clouds. Lightning flickered in the distance and thunder quietly rumbled.

Alan had finished his shift steering the barge, and now it was Paul's turn. The man took to it naturally, easily avoiding the riverbanks. Amanda and Eric sat nearby.

The barge rounded a bend, and an abandoned dock area with a loading crane and several sunken supply boats came into view. Suddenly, a familiar jingle pierced the darkness. Muffled but unmistakable came the sounds that could only mean Kirby Paint and Tile Plus—in Westgate.

Alan tensed. The Kirbys exchanged looks of panic, then scanned the shore.

"My sat-phone," Paul whispered.

"The Spinosaurus," Eric said.

Alan went to the barge's rail. "Keep quiet."

Paul cut the motor. The barge continued downstream and the ringing grew louder.

Alan's eyes widened at the sight of seven mounds of dinosaur dung sitting on a patch of treeless, flat ground just beyond the riverbank. He looked to the Kirbys. An idea came to all of them at once.

"Find it before it stops ringing!" Alan said.

Amanda, Paul, and Alan jumped into the river and rushed to the bank. Eric was about to leap into the water when his mother raised her hand.

"Eric Kirby!" she called. "You stay right where you are! I'm still your mother!"

"Keep watch for us, son," Paul added.

The boy nodded.

Alan, Amanda, and Paul sprinted toward the dark heaps.

Alan held his breath as he plunged his arms into the closest mound of dinosaur dung. The stench was overwhelming!

"I've got something!" Paul said as he dug into another pile. "I think I've got something!"

Alan watched Eric's father withdraw a pager.

"Over here!" Amanda yelled. She was covered in dino dung, just like Alan and Paul.

The still-ringing phone was in her hand. Alan

grabbed the phone from Amanda and answered it.

"You, too, can own a time-share in beautiful Guadalajara . . . ," a recorded voice said.

Alan shut off the phone. He was about to turn when he saw Eric waving madly from the barge.

"Behind you!" Eric screamed.

Alan slowly turned. A fierce, twenty-foot-long, red-and-black-scaled, horned Carnotaurus stood directly before the trio. It was smaller than a rex, but still big enough to devour them. The dinosaur's eyes were pitch-black, its arms were tiny, its body and tail stout. Its maw was filled with bladelike teeth. It drooled at the sight of them.

Grrrrhhhh-rggggghhhhhlll!

It sniffed. Once. Twice. Then again.

Bllll-eahhhhh!

With a look of distaste, it walked away. It seemed that even a Carnotaurus had its standards, and meat covered in dung was not on its menu for the evening.

"Can't help but be a little offended," Paul said.

Moments later, Alan and the others were back on the barge. Paul pointed out the dock they had spotted and aimed the barge for it. Amanda began fiercely scrubbing herself off.

"Do you think that's a good idea?" Eric asked his mother. "I think I should swim over and cover myself in that stuff. That way, maybe the dinosaurs won't want to . . . you know—"

"I'm not gonna be stinking of this," Amanda said. "And neither is my son—or my husband."

Eric caught another odd look pass between his parents. It seemed to him that the crisis was bringing his mother and father together.

Maybe there was hope for the Kirby family after all, thought Eric. *If* they could just get off this island!

The phone was still in Alan's hands. The battery-level indicator was flashing. Its charge was running down.

"Whatever you do, don't call the U.S. Embassy," advised Paul. "They won't do a thing."

"Well, we don't exactly have a Costa Rican phone book here," said Alan. "So it will have to be somebody we know in the States. Someone we can absolutely count on to send help."

"My brother Stan," Paul said.

"I wouldn't trust Stan to find a snowball in a blizzard," Amanda said.

Paul looked at her, then shrugged and nodded. It seemed like she had a point.

"What's that?" asked Eric, pointing toward the murky water. Just below the surface, a shimmering wave of silver passed beneath the boat. A single fish jumped from the water. Then another.

"Bonitos," Alan said.

"Something must have scared them," said Eric, tensing. He met Alan's eyes. Eric had learned the hard way that nature had many warning signs. They were seeing one now.

Thunder sounded again. This time, much closer.

"Get the motor going," Alan called to Paul, who nodded and tried to start the engine. It sputtered but would not turn over.

The phone beeped to indicate that the battery was getting even weaker. Alan closed his eyes and made a decision, then quickly dialed a familiar number.

"Who are you calling?" Amanda asked.

Alan ignored the question. The line rang three times. Four. Finally, someone answered.

"Hewwo?" a little boy said.

Alan knew the voice. "Charlie, get your mother. Right away!"

A long silence followed.

"Charlie, are you there?" Alan asked. He looked around anxiously.

"Hewwo?" Charlie repeated.

The phone beeped again. The battery was dangerously low now. Behind Alan, Paul continued to struggle with the motor.

"Charlie! It's the dinosaur man!" Alan cried into the phone. "Go get Mommy, okay?"

"Okay," said Charlie. The sound came of the phone being dropped onto a table.

Amanda and Eric watched Alan. They all knew their lives could be riding on this single phone call.

Suddenly, something distracted Eric. As he looked toward the bow, his body tensed and he called, "Dr. Grant!"

The phone pressed tightly to his ear, Alan turned and saw a gigantic fin rise from the water fifty feet behind them. It was heading right for them!

"Charlie? Charlie!" Alan yelled in desperation. "Are you getting Mommy? *Charlie!*"

With shattering force, the boat was rammed and everyone was sent tumbling! Alan slammed against the wheelhouse support bar. The phone slipped from his hand and fell to the deck, landing on the "end call" button. The connection was severed.

As lightning flashed and thunder roared, the Spinosaurus rose out of the dark water, its massive form towering over the barge.

RRRRHHH-AWWWHHHRRR!

Long crocodile-shaped jaws lunged toward Alan, who had only one thought before leaping away with all his strength—*Never underestimate the reach of a superpredator!*

He got clear, just barely.

The massive jaws connected with the barge instead. Then the Spinosaurus ripped the entire wheelhouse from the deck.

It started on the stern next, puncturing the fuel tank, clearly enjoying its little destructive fest. Fuel leaked into the river, spreading into a large slick.

Alan rushed toward the front of the craft. He herded the Kirbys into the dinosaur cage that had been left on the barge. He jumped in, too, and closed the door.

With any luck, the cage's bars would be strong enough to protect them, like a shark cage in unfriendly waters.

But the Spinosaurus's rampage near the stern made the entire craft unstable. When the dinosaur lifted the back of the boat from the water, the cage slid across the deck and slammed into the bow.

Alan realized that the cage door was pinned shut. They were trapped. Debris and pieces of abandoned equipment slid forward as the Spinosaurus lifted its end of the boat even higher.

Alan gasped as he saw the phone among the junk sliding toward oblivion—and heard it start to ring!

Reaching through the cage bars for the sliding

phone, Alan strained until his arm felt as if it might tear from its socket.

The Spinosaurus dropped the barge and the phone slid back toward the stern again!

Alan saw the dinosaur's jagged maw approaching. The cage was their only protection now. The dinosaur's teeth fastened on it, lifting it a few feet from the deck. Alan and the others were knocked around like rag dolls as the cage was smashed back down.

The ringing phone flew through the air. Alan lunged for it, shouting in triumph as his fingers closed on the prize.

GRAGHHHHH-RAGHHHHH!

Furiously, the Spinosaurus battered the boat, sinking the barge, cage and all, into the river. As the icy water rose in the cage, Alan frantically pressed the phone's "talk" button.

"ELLIE!" screamed Alan, praying it was her. Praying she had caller ID or star-six-nine or some other blasted form of suburban tele-technology that would give her a clue he was reliving his worst nightmare!

"Alan?" Ellie said. "Alan, is that—"

The deafening roar of the Spinosaurus came again, drowning out Ellie's voice.

The water was now up to Alan's neck. He pressed his face against the bars and kept the phone just over the waterline. The Kirbys struggled beside him.

"ELLIE!" Alan hollered. "SITE B, ELLIE! THE RIVER—"

Then the water closed over Alan like a fist. He jammed the phone into his waistband and held his breath as he and Paul tugged desperately on the cage door. All four were running out of air as the cage suffered another jarring impact. Their world tilted to one side and they rose up, as if they were being hauled by an insane machine.

The Spinosaurus lifted the cage out of the river in its powerful jaws. It shook the cage, trying to find a way in. As the cage toppled, its door swung open and Paul flew out, splashing into the river. He surfaced, out of breath and disoriented.

Alan, Amanda, and Eric weren't so lucky. Still trapped in the cage, Amanda screamed as the dinosaur turned the cage upright and reached inside with its long clawed arms. Eric screamed with her as a giant killing claw nearly ripped his shirt.

Alan tried desperately to think of something to do, but his mind was stricken with terror.

In seconds, they would all be eaten.

Near the dock, Paul watched in horror as the Spinosaurus attacked the cage full of food.

Food.

His family was *food* to this thing!

Paul felt his entire body shudder, but he couldn't escape the truth: *No one can save my family now but me.*

Paul climbed halfway up the abandoned crane arm. He waved frantically and yelled, "Hey! Hey! OVER HERE! HEEEEEYYY!"

The dinosaur turned, the cage still in its grip, and grunted at the sight of Paul, as vulnerable as a worm on a fishhook.

RAHHHHGHHHHHHHH!!!

The dinosaur cast the cage aside and came after him.

"That's right, come on, ya big wussbag!" Paul hollered. With shaking hands, he climbed even higher.

Eric was afraid.

He'd stayed alive for eight weeks. Managed not to get eaten, or poisoned, or ripped apart. But what did that matter? Now he was facing something more frightening than drowning or being eaten.

He was about to see his own father torn apart by a ravenous predator.

"Dad!" Eric screamed.

Then he felt Alan's hand grasping the back of his shirt. The scientist practically dragged Eric and his equally panicked mother to the shore.

Alan watched as his father climbed higher and higher up the crane arm, narrowly avoiding the Spinosaurus as it reached for him.

"All right, Dad!" Eric yelled. "Keep going!"

Enraged, the Spinosaurus clutched the steel lattice of the arm and rocked the unstable structure back and forth. Dangling fifty feet over the water, Paul was slung side to side.

"Run!" Paul shouted to his family. "Amanda, get Eric away!"

Eric looked to his mother, who seemed to have no idea how to make this impossible choice. Her husband—or her son?

Eric made the decision for her. "We're staying. We're gonna help Dad!"

The only question was how.

Alan spotted a shiny object among the debris from the boat. It was a flare gun, with spare flares attached to the handle.

Picking up the gun, Alan slammed a flare into it. He tried to aim for the dinosaur's head, but the blasted thing was moving so fast he was sure he'd miss.

Then he sniffed the fuel that had spilled over the water and another idea came to him. He aimed the gun at the fuel slick and fired.

WHOOOOOSH!

The river ignited! The Spinosaurus roared as flames shot up around it. It flailed, slamming with incredible force into the crane arm. Then it fled, disappearing into the jungle on the far side of the river.

Alan and Eric watched in horror as Paul, still clinging to the toppling arm, rode it into the sea of fire below.

"Paul!" Amanda shouted.

"Dad!" Eric yelled. "DAD!"

Alan, Amanda, and Eric called for Paul, but the only sound was the crackling flames along the water.

"No," Amanda said. "Oh, no. Please, please, no . . ."

"DAAAD!" Eric screamed. "DAAAD!"

Eric and Amanda's anguished cries echoed in the night. Alan turned away.

"We should keep moving," he said. "That thing could circle back."

"No," Eric said firmly. "No! We can't leave Dad."

Eric's mother knelt down and faced him. "Let me tell you a few things about your dad, okay? He's very, very clever, very, very brave, and he loves you very, very much."

Eric blinked. His mother hadn't said two nice

words about his dad in months—maybe even *years*.

"He loves *you*, too, you know?" Eric told his mother pointedly. It was time she realized that.

"Okay," she agreed. "He loves *us* very, very much. And I know that right now more than anything, your dad would want to know that we're safe. Okay?"

Eric nodded. But it was a sad nod. What was he going to do without his dad? He suddenly felt more lost and alone than he had in all the weeks he'd spent isolated on this island.

"We're going to get out of this," said Amanda, but tears were in her eyes, too. "Everything's going to be all right, I promise."

Suddenly, a sound came from behind them. A crunch of sand. Eric tensed.

Was it another predator?

"Listen to your mother," a voice called from over Eric's shoulder.

Eric turned. Out of the darkness stepped Paul Kirby.

Eric ran straight into his father's arms.

"Good thing I've been swimming at the Y, huh?" Paul joked.

As tears spilled from Amanda's eyes, she hugged her husband and her son as if she'd never again let them go.

CHAPTER 13

AT DAWN, ALAN LED THE GROUP in a hike along the river. They were exhausted, but trying to keep their spirits up.

"You remember when we went fishing last summer?" Paul asked his son. "And I was trying to put the boat in the water and the trailer sank? And then the tow truck came and tried to pull it out but got dragged in? And the truck driver threatened to knock your dad's lights out? So I said I was the governor, and he believed me?"

"Yeah," said Eric with a laugh.

"That was a fun day," said Paul.

Amanda gazed at her laughing son and her smiling husband. "We should try fishing again," she told them.

"You mean it?" asked Paul.

"I do. It's worth another shot," Amanda said, looking into her husband's eyes. "Who knows? Things could turn out differently."

Eric saw his mother take his father's hand. *There's my cue to take a hike,* Eric decided, seeing Alan take the same cue by moving ahead. *After all, a guy's got to know when to give his parents some privacy.*

Eric jogged to catch up with Alan.

"The lady you called, how do you know she can help us?" Eric asked the scientist.

"She's one person I could always count on," Alan said. "And she's saved me more times than she realizes. I owe her everything."

They walked together in silence, Alan considering his words.

"It strikes me now I never told her that," Alan finally admitted.

"You should," Eric said.

Alan nodded. "You're right."

A sound drifted their way. A low murmur. A soft, familiar rush and a lazy crashing of waves.

"Do you hear that?" Alan asked.

Eric nodded excitedly. "It's the ocean."

Alan called to the Kirbys and all four ran onward. Soon they emerged from the jungle into an area of thinner trees and sand. Rocky outcroppings dotted the landscape. The piercing cry of gulls rose over the gentle sounds of the surf.

Suddenly, Alan noticed a shadow fall over the group. He tensed as several other shadows joined it—thirty-foot shadows.

Cahhhhhrrrrrr!

A flock of Pteranodons had dropped from the sky and were now landing in front of Alan and the Kirbys. Several had auburn wings. One had gray wings and an orange-and-black-striped head. It was the Pteranodon that had snatched Eric up and taken him to its nest!

The giant reptile lurched nightmarishly toward Eric, but his mother stepped in front of him. The Pteranodon advanced on her in a blur. Before it could strike, Paul leaped onto the Pteranodon's back, grabbing its pointed crest. He wrestled with the fierce predator to keep its stabbing beak away from his wife.

Flapping its wings and spinning without warning, the giant Pteranodon flung Paul to the sand. Other Pteranodons whipped their wings excitedly as they prepared to join the attack.

Alan looked for a tree branch, a rock, anything he could use for a weapon.

Suddenly, an alien but oddly familiar sound pierced the air. Then blurs of yipping, howling, furious motion raced in from every direction.

Raptors!

The Pteranodons shrieked in rage, as if they were meeting an ancient enemy last encountered 65 million years ago!

Eric saw two raptors move in front of the others. They were bigger, clearly the pack leaders. The alpha male had a smoky gray stripe that lined its entire body, right down to the tip of its tail. The alpha female had jagged diamond-shaped patterns running along its flank and rubylike scales dotting the depressions of its eye sockets.

The alpha male leaped into the air, bringing down the giant Pteranodon as it tried to escape.

Chaos erupted around Alan and the Kirbys.

A trio of Pteranodons swooped down and seized the alpha male raptor, lifting it! The giant Pteranodon fought its way free of the melee and rose into the sky, circling and cawing. The airborne combatants rose higher and soon disappeared over the tree line.

"This way!" Alan yelled. "Quick!"

He led the group away from the battle, toward a barren knoll. Eric could see blue water ahead. The edge of Isla Sorna was in sight. All that stood between them and the ocean was twenty feet of sand and—

Yip! Yip! HISSSSS-YIEEEEE!

A dozen raptors charged in and circled the group.

There was nowhere to run. Eric's parents and Alan huddled around him, trying to protect him, but Eric knew it was no use. The raptors would shred them all in seconds.

Yet—the raptors didn't attack.

Eric stared into the eyes of the closest raptor. *They want something from us,* Eric realized.

"The eggs," Alan said. "They want the eggs. Otherwise we'd be dead already."

With painstaking care, Alan eased the pack off his shoulder. He opened it, reached inside, and pulled out the camera bag. As he did, he spotted something else in the pack—the cast of the raptor resonating chamber. Days ago he'd put it in his pack and forgotten about it!

The circle of raptors broke ranks, and slowly the alpha female raptor approached. Closer and closer, she came. She circled the humans, raising and lowering her head as if with some grave purpose.

"Everyone, get down!" Alan said. "She's challenging us!"

Eric and the others dropped to their knees.

The alpha female stopped before Eric's mother. The dinosaur leaned forward, until it was inches away from Amanda's face. The woman trembled.

"She thinks I did it," Amanda said. "She thinks I stole the eggs!"

Paul tried to edge his way in front of his wife, but the alpha female raptor barked once and snarled at Paul.

"Give me the eggs," Amanda said.

With extreme care, Alan handed the eggs to Amanda. She set them down in the sand.

The raptors became agitated. Some tensed, as if ready to launch into a killing frenzy. Others trembled and looked to one another for guidance.

Suddenly, an eerie sound filled the air.

Hrrrrrr-rreeeee!

Everyone turned to look at Alan, who held the cast of the raptor resonating chamber near his mouth. He was trying to communicate with the raptors!

With a deep, shaky breath, he blew through it once more, creating the same eerie pitch that he'd heard the raptors make.

Hrrrrrr-rreeeee! Hrrrrrr-rreeeee!

The alpha female studied Alan closely. How could this creature be making the sound of their tribe?

A single male raptor started forward. The alpha female barked a sharp command. Cowed, the male backed away, unwilling to challenge the authority of the alpha female.

Alan blew into the cast again. The raptors bayed in confusion.

This was a cry for help, Eric thought. A sign made only by a fellow raptor. He'd heard it many times in his eight weeks on the island.

The alpha female suddenly swung around toward the coast. All the raptors fell silent, as if they could hear something the humans could not.

Then the sound drifted in. A distant thrumming. The sound of the keepers, the makers, the humans who had raised and caged these animals.

The alpha female barked twice and quickly picked up one of the eggs. The male who had advanced before came forward and picked up the other one.

The circle of raptors broke. One by one the nervous predators leaped into the jungle—and were gone.

As Eric's parents hugged their son close, Alan stood and let out a shaky sigh of relief.

Suddenly, a new sound pierced the air. A voice on a bullhorn. "Dr. Grant!"

"It's coming from the ocean," Alan said. He rushed over the rise, Eric and his parents right behind him.

Eric couldn't believe what he was looking at. A man in a business suit stood in the sand.

"Dr. Grant?" the man asked through a bullhorn in his hand.

The battle-weary foursome charged out of the scrub, waving their arms and yelling.

"That bullhorn is a very *bad* idea!" Paul and Amanda told the man at once.

What they saw next stopped them in their tracks. Eric's eyes widened.

A massive military presence sat off the coast. Eric counted half a dozen U.S. Navy warships. A helicopter gunship rested on the beach, rotors still turning.

"Whoa," Eric said. Then he laughed as he saw his mother and father embrace, then kiss.

Eric walked beside Alan toward the military rescue party.

"Dr. Grant, that friend you called?" Eric said. "You have to thank her now. She sent the navy *and* the marines!"

"Bless you, Ellie," Alan whispered.

Inside the chopper, Dr. Alan Grant experienced the shock of his life. A heavily bandaged figure lay upon a stretcher, his face turned toward the light streaming in from outside.

"Billy!" Alan cried.

Billy's hand weakly rose. Alan rushed forward and clasped it.

"Glad to see you, Billy," Alan said. His voice was choked with emotion. "You're a good man.

I'm so sorry this happened to you."

Billy smiled. "Are you kidding?" he said hoarsely. "You know the kind of great stories I'll be able to tell now? Hey, it was worth it. Oh, and one more thing . . . I saved your hat."

Shaking his head, Alan smiled, seeing the battered fedora on the floor next to the stretcher. "Well, that's the important thing, isn't it?"

A medic eased Billy's head back. The young man's eyes fluttered and he drifted off to sleep.

"He's lost a lot of blood, but he's going to make it," the medic said.

Alan nodded. He strapped himself in with the Kirbys and leaned back, relaxing for the first time in days as the chopper lifted into the air.

Eric sat nestled between his parents. He looked to Billy, then to Alan, who smiled and nodded.

Turning to the window, Eric looked out on the island, his mind filled with unanswerable questions. He had come here a boy filled with dreams of adventure. What he had experienced had changed him. Could he exist in the world outside again? Or would his dreams be filled with this island for the rest of his life?

Suddenly, the pilot shouted, "Hostile! Nine o'clock!"

The two military pilots in the cabin snapped to

action as a Pteranodon dropped into view through the window. Eric gasped, startled at the sight of the reptile flying alongside them.

"One at three!" a marine said. He raised the barrel of his rifle and took careful aim.

"No!" Alan yelled. He grabbed the rifle's barrel and pointed it away. "They're just flying in formation. They think we're one of them."

Eric watched as a third Pteranodon joined the other auburn-winged flyers, forming the point of a V. As horrifying as the creatures had been moments ago, they were suddenly beautiful again. Each of their giant wings beat a delicate rhythm unlike anything Eric could ever have imagined.

Soon the leader of the Pteranodons banked right, pulling away from the helicopter. The others followed it. Only—

They didn't fly back to the island.

Eric watched as the Pteranodons sailed off. He spoke to Alan without shifting his gaze.

"Pteranodons in the Mesozoic could fly over oceans and go from one continent to another. Where do you think these are heading?"

"I don't know. Maybe to find a new nesting ground," Alan said. "It's a whole new world for them."

"I dare them to nest in Enid, Oklahoma," Amanda said.

Paul looked over. He took his wife's hand. "Let's go home."

Eric smiled. He had almost given up hope— even before the accident that stranded him on the island—that he would ever have a place to call home again.

Now he knew everything would be all right.

Alan looked up as the copilot handed him a pair of headsets.

"For you," the copilot said.

Alan put them on, adjusting the microphone. He had to yell over the noise of the chopper.

"This is Grant," Alan said.

"Alan?" Ellie asked. "Alan! Are you okay?"

"Ellie! Yes! I'm fine." He was grinning like a schoolboy.

"I don't believe you," Ellie said. "You told me a paleontologist had no business being on that island."

"I know."

"So what were you doing?" Ellie asked.

Alan leaned back and allowed the golden sunlight to wash over him. "Evolving."

He gazed out the window, taking in the primal

beauty of the Pteranodons. They were flying northward, beside the sunrise.

It was a new dawn, a new beginning, and Alan Grant didn't look away. He kept watching, even after the fluttering silhouettes dissolved in the shimmering light.

Do you wonder how thirteen-year-old Eric Kirby
stayed alive for eight weeks *alone*
in Jurassic Park?

Read Eric's harrowing survival story
in the original novel

SURVIVOR

by Scott Ciencin,
the first in the new
Jurassic Park™
Adventures
series from Boxtree,
Universal Studios,
and Amblin Entertainment.

ISBN: 0 7522 1978 2
Available now!

Don't miss the next Jurassic Park™ Adventure!

PREY
By Scott Ciencin

A band of teenagers armed with video cameras
and what they think are "the rules of the island"
invade Jurassic Park. But their dream of making
a blockbuster dinosaur documen-
tary soon turns into a nightmare
because dinosaurs don't play by
anyone's rules. Can paleontologist
Dr. Alan Grant and thirteen-year-
old Eric Kirby save them? Or will
they all become prey?

Coming November 2001
ISBN: 0 7522 1979 0

ABOUT THE AUTHOR

SCOTT CIENCIN is a best-selling author of adult and children's fiction. Praised by *Science Fiction Review* as "one of today's finest fantasy writers," and listed in *The Encyclopedia of Fantasy*, Scott has written over forty works, many published by Warner, Avon, and TSR. For Random House Children's Publishing, Scott is now writing the Jurassic Park™ Adventures series. He is also a favorite author in the popular Dinotopia series, for which he's written six titles: *Windchaser, Lost City, Thunder Falls, Sky Dance, Return to Lost City,* and *The Explorers.*

Among Scott's other recent projects is the children's series Dinoverse, a six-book fantasy adventure that takes readers on an exciting and humorous journey through the Age of Dinosaurs. Scott's Dinoverse titles include: *I Was a Teenage T. Rex* (#1), *The Teens Time Forgot* (#2), *Raptor Without a Cause* (#3), *Please Don't Eat the Teacher!* (#4), *Beverly Hills Brontosaurus* (#5), and *Dinosaurs Ate My Homework* (#6).

Scott has also directed for television and scripted comic books. He lives in Florida with his wife, Denise.